TAMANNA

SHIVANI MISHRA

ISBN 979-8-89066-914-8

CONTENTS

PROLOGUE

Love and *Hate* were sitting adjacent to each other in front of a bonfire. *Love* was a bit preoccupied, while *Hate* found the crackling of fire very intriguing. After some time, *Love* asked *Hate*, "Why do people have more affinity for you than for me?"

Hate replied, "Probably because I'm easier and much less complex."

Peace and *War* were sitting at the dining table, each engrossed in its own reverie. Breaking the silence of the table and the fantasies of their reveries, *Peace* asked *War*, "If people want me, why do they approach you first? You are not my assistant!" To which *War* replied, "Perhaps I am more easily available than you."

1990

Who am I? Tamanna.

How old am I? Nine years old.

Where do I live? It's a village. Sometimes there is peace here; other times hatred and violence.

What about my family? A submissive and docile mother; a customarily inebriated and abusive father; two elder brothers (eighteen and eleven years old respectively), one, who had sworn upon his life to be another version of his father, and the other had pledged to be a nuisance to the world; one elder sister (fifteen years old), a figure of love and protection for me; and my grandparents, who seemed to have nothing to do in life but sleep, eat, abuse my mother, my sister and me, dote on my two brothers and worship my father. Not that they were unaware of my father's nature, nor were they blind or deaf; only that they had covered their eyes with a cloth that had blurred their vision and severed any connection between right and wrong.

What are my hobbies? Playing with my friends Eva, Eric, Nazia, Taheera and Vihaan; talking to my sister; reading, jumping, running around, singing, dancing and whatnot! I love going to school too. Why? Because I love the library and I can read there all day, spend time with my friends and stay away from my house.

Why do I want to stay away from my house? Simply because it is a house and not a *home*.

Do you want to know a bit about my friends? Eva and Eric are twins who live in the village adjacent to ours; Nazia and Taheera live in the village opposite ours, while Vihaan lives a few houses away from mine. For some reason, quite unknown and unfathomable to me, these three villages are always in conflict with each other, especially mine, and Nazia and Taheera's. All six of us have been inseparable since the time we've known the meanings of friendship, family, loneliness and the compelling desire for congruous company. Our friendship was never accepted by our villagers, and will probably never be. But what do a bunch of six to nine-year-olds care about the villagers and their opinions? We have fought with our families, our villagers, and our relatives, and have always emerged victorious (even if slightly bruised). I don't know what holds the six of us together. It's probably the solicitude and familial feeling that we can't find within our own families.

2019

Times have changed. My life has changed – from spending the first half in a house which undermined hell to spending the second half in a cage.

The inclination of these times is beyond my comprehension. With time, questions have also changed – if not completely – and their answers too.

What's my name? Tamanna.

Who am I? A daughter, a sister, a wife, a mother to two children, a professor, a philanthropist, a writer, and above all, a *human*. We often tend to miss out on this last point of our identity.

What's my religion? I am an atheist.

What's my political ideology? Not relevant.

Which country do I belong to? I belong to this world.

Where do I live? It's a city. Sometimes, there is peace here; other times hatred and violence. The name of the city is irrelevant.

How did I get married? I had an arranged marriage at the age of eighteen. I had barely known my husband when I got married to him. In fact, it was on the day of my wedding that I first talked to him. I was going through a plethora of emotions after the wedding was over. I was nervous; I was scared; I was infuriated; I was sad. Most of all, I felt helpless; since my childhood, I had seen that once a girl gets married, she can do absolutely nothing with her life. Her life ends when she is born; she dies a second time when she is married off. But I was unaware that life had something else in store for me.

Who comprises my present family? My husband, who has been the strongest pillar of my life; and two lovely and doting children – a son who is thirteen years old and a daughter, ten years old.

How did my previous life shape my present life? That's a long, dramatic story.

1988 – NEW RELATIONS

Under normal circumstances and in normal households, children wake up to soft nudges and sweet voices calling out their names in melodic tunes, but my family wasn't "normal." That day, I woke up to screaming, shouting, yelling and seeing my father, drunk, incessantly slapping my mother and hurling abuses at her, at his life, at his fate; then at objects in the house, like the chair beside him, at the mat under his feet (which, at one point, tried to pull him to the ground, and might have led him to break his hip into pieces, left him in pain and me, content), at the glass of water kept beside my grandparents' mattress, and everything else that his eyes could see and the air could touch. Interestingly, my father possessed a wide variety of abuses – the number easily exceeding the average alcoholic content in his blood.

I rubbed my eyes and woke up from the cold, mud floor; I folded the sheet, kept it in the rack and quietly hopped out of the window under which I made my bed every day. That window had become my lifesaver – my usual escape route when the main door was blocked by my father's antics. I'd regularly find myself in situations where escape was the only path towards sanity and peace. So, despite my young age, I had become skilled at the craft of escaping.

I went to the well near our house and splashed some fresh, clean water on my face. Since it was no use going back to that assault-and-alcohol-strained house, I decided to take a stroll in our village. It was a chilly winter morning, and I was wearing only a thin, worn-out sweater with holes scattered all along its surface as a shield from the biting winds. I could see the mountain peak at some distance, golden, with the sun's rays embracing it. The sun hadn't come out yet; it was only peeking through the peak of the mountain. Some houses were still under the blanket of the cold sleep that had draped them the previous night. My hands and ears, completely uncovered, were left at the mercy of the freezing winds. No matter how much I rubbed my hands against each other and touched them to my ears, I could feel the last traces of sensation leaving my body.

After walking for a few more metres, I heard a vague sound of two children laughing. I halted and swerved in all directions to find where the sound of laughter was coming from. It intrigued me to know that there were two more children out of their homes so early in the morning. I kept following the sound without paying any heed that I had left my village behind and was heading towards the common mango tree that was shared by us with two more villages.

"Hey!" I shouted, standing just below the tree. "Who are you?"

I could see a boy and a girl, perched up high in the tree. They seemed to be approximately my age, but it was primarily their clothes that helped me distinguish between the girl and the boy.

"We should be asking that question to you! You interrupted our discussion," the boy shouted back.

"Well, you appeared to be more engrossed in laughing than in any sort of discussion," I retorted.

"Then, why did you intrude while we were laughing?"

"Shut up, Eric!" the girl exclaimed. "Do you always have to be so argumentative? Keep quiet and let me talk to her," she commanded. She turned towards me and said, "Hey! My name's Eva, and he is my brother, Eric." Even though she was talking pretty loudly, her voice still carried a hint of affection and warmth. "What's your name?" she further added.

"I am Tamanna. What are you two doing on that tree so early in the morning?"

"Oh! This is our favourite place. We come here whenever we feel frustrated or dismal. What about you?"

"I was just wandering in the village. What did you say after 'frustrated or…?'"

"Dismal."

"What does that mean?"

She had begun to explain to me the meaning of that word when I heard the coarse voice of my eldest brother, Rahul.

"Tamanna! What are you doing here?" He came striding towards me, his hands rolled into tight fists, the veins of his arms almost popping out. He held me by my arm tightly and, glowering down at me, asked, "Why did you leave the house without informing anyone? Do you have any idea how worried everyone is?"

"Really? As if my staying in the house makes any difference to anyone!" I mocked.

"Shut up!" he shouted and pulled me up so that I was then standing on my toes.

"Let go! You are hurting me!" I cried.

"Then, you should consider keeping your trap shut," he replied with gritted teeth. He started pulling me away while I relentlessly implored him to release my hand.

5

AN UNAVOIDABLE REALITY

When we reached our house and were just outside the entrance, my brother said in a hushed tone, "We have guests. They have come to discuss Durga's marriage. Behave properly in front of them and don't you dare be yourself."

"What do you mean by 'don't be yourself?'" I asked, agitated.

"I mean wild, shameless and a brat." I frowned at him and was about to retort when he pulled me in.

The scene that I witnessed left me mildly perplexed. My mother was frantically scurrying around in the kitchen, making tea, gathering snacks, frying *pakoras* and arranging all these on a large plate which I had never seen before (I asked her later what that plate was, and she said that it was called a 'tray.') And my grandparents? I couldn't even recognise them! The usually grotesque scarecrows had suddenly turned into melodious nightingales! I had never seen them smile as widely and congenially as they were then. The glaring feint would have been visible to anyone who knew the two scarecrows. My father was nowhere to be seen, which did not surprise me. My sister, Durga Di was helping my mother and bore a nervous expression. My second brother, Naveen, was sitting in front of the guests, clearly awkward and clueless.

Coming on to the guests – the primary reason behind this chaotic transformation. Considering our acute financial conditions in those days, the next in line to derive our services and oblations after God were the rich landlords and *zamindars*. But they seemed to me to be neither God nor rich landlords. In fact, they looked as penniless and destitute as us. There was a woman, a man about the same age as my parents and two boys. One seemed to be my age and the other would have been in his mid-twenties. The man and the woman – who were a couple in all probability – looked more complacent and pompous than their social status should have allowed, and sat with an utterly disgruntled attitude. Their eyes kept wandering away, as though looking for someone, someone capable enough of rescuing them from frivolous people such as us. The older boy appeared to be petrified and absolutely displeased with his and his family's presence in our house.

'*Ohhh... So, THIS is the boy*,' I thought. It was evident by his face that the marriage was happening despite his discontent. The reason for this nonconformity did not capture my curiosity at that moment. Principally, it was the younger boy who caught my gaze, probably because he evinced the same confusion that I felt internally. All the fuss and importance he found himself engulfed in was beyond his discernment too. He smiled sheepishly when he saw me staring at him.

"She is our youngest sister, Tamanna," my brother informed them.

"Does she always wander away early in the morning without telling anyone?" the woman asked haughtily.

"No. Only when I feel like." I tried to be as precise as I could.

"Keep quiet," my grandmother hissed at me. She turned to the woman, her countenance changing rapidly from outright hatred to genuine pretence, and said, "Forgive her. She is just a child. She isn't normally so straightforward, but you know the children these days."

"Yes, I do, and it will do you good if you know how to deal with girls such as her. It won't be long before she grows wings and is out of your grasp." I had opened my mouth to reply but one glare from my mother was enough to keep my impulse in check.

"Please help yourselves," my mother urged them, keeping the tray full of mouth-watering dishes in front of them.

"Will I get any?" I asked excitedly. Even though it wasn't an unusual question, coming from a five-year-old, it did invite some spiteful and insatiate glances from the woman.

"You will. Later," my mother replied curtly.

"Why? There are so many! She can have some from this plate," the boy said and held out the plate towards me. As I was about to take a *pakora* from that plate, the woman slapped me on my hand.

"Don't you have any manners at all?" she bellowed. "And you," she said turning towards her son, "Who asked you to be so generous? If you don't want to eat, leave it as it is."

"Sorry, Ma," the boy said timidly, his face lowered, and his chin almost touching his chest.

That night, I lay in bed, thinking. My sister was lying beside me, facing me and I could see that she was awake too.

"*Didi*, what's the name of the boy?"

"Rihan."

"Why did you look so unhappy?"

"Probably because I am in the same situation in which Ma was a few years back."

"And what's that?"

"Go off to sleep, Tamanna." With that, she turned to the other side and dozed off.

A year later, I realised that nothing productive had resulted from that meeting. It was the wedding day, and I could see my sister's swollen red eyes. Vihaan ("the boy" and also my newfound friend along with Eva and Eric) had told me all about his brother's resistance and defiance, his parents' stubbornness, the brutal beating and his own fear of separation from his beloved elder brother. In that one year, I had heard about and interacted with him enough to know that Rihan Bhaiya was an individual with his own set of morals. His protests were not out of dislike towards our family or contempt for my sister; it was out of the fear and anxiety of letting go of his long-nurtured dreams and losing his principles to his parents' mindless insistence. It was out of a feeling of helplessness in being unable to abide by his own beliefs. It was out of the horror of chaining a girl's whole life in yet another house.

6

NEW RELATIONS

Vihaan, Eva, Eric and I soon developed a solid bond. Our days started with each other and ended with each other. We shared everything with each other; from the colour of the butterfly that we had seen a while ago on our way to the mango tree, to the slightest bit of insult we'd had to endure from our families; there was nothing that we hid from each other or did not talk about.

One day, when the four of us were sitting under the mango tree, reviving our breath after running and chasing one another for almost an hour, we heard the sound of scared, muffled sobs not far from the tree. We divided ourselves in four directions and went on a search mission to find the source of these sobs.

After looking around for about half a minute, Eric called out, "Here!"

We ran towards him; he was standing in front of a bush which could have been a potential hiding place for two to three grown men. What greeted us was actually the apprehension and torment of two girls at being discovered. They seemed to be sisters, their faces smeared with tears. The older one had squeezed the younger one in a tight, protective hug, which was, in turn, reciprocated. The younger one clutched her sister even more tightly upon seeing us.

"Hello! Who are you? And what are you doing here?" I asked politely, crouching towards them.

"I won't tell you! What if you go and tell them that we're hiding here?" the older one retorted with a quivering voice.

"Why are you hiding? Are you thieves?" Eric asked in his usual straightforward manner.

"Try keeping your mouth shut sometimes, Eric," Eva said, glaring at Eric. She crouched down beside me and said in a sweet voice, "We won't tell anyone. You can trust us. We've been in this same situation as you are in right now at some point or the other in our lives." We helped them come out of the bush and settled them under the mango tree. The younger girl was still clasping her elder sister tightly.

"Tell us what happened," I said, softly.

"Our father and uncles want to beat us up," the elder one replied, still nervous.

"For?"

"For demanding education."

"What? You haven't gone to a school before?" Eric asked.

"No. The women in our family are not supposed to be educated."

"But aren't you a girl?"

"If you do not shut up right now, you won't be able to call yourself a *human* ever again," Eva threatened Eric.

"Well, I don't think it's that big an issue," Eva said, turning towards the two girls. "Even our families don't prioritise our education, especially mine and Tamanna's."

"But they never threatened to kill you because you wanted to go to school, did they?" This question silenced us. No matter how different all of us were, we loved going to school. We were curious about every little thing; from the leaf falling on the ground to the varying human behaviour. And somehow, we felt that the more we studied, the closer it took us to our innumerable answers. We loved going to school also because it gave us an opportunity to get out of our houses and forget about our families for some time. The four of us never knew what a peaceful family looked like, or whether it even existed or not. Probably this is why the knowledge of these two girls staying in their houses all through the day was almost revolting.

"Sorry. We weren't aware of that," Eva said, searching for the right words. This was unlike Eva; she always knew what to say. She was good with people and with words.

"But you need not worry!" I chimed in. "We won't tell on you. Our situations are pretty similar, if not identical. We loathe our families too. In fact, we see each other's faces more than we see our families.'"

"Really?" the older girl asked, incredulous, but slightly hesitant.

"Yes. You can confide in us," Eva reassured, with her usual sweet smile.

"YES," the rest three of us chorused.

Just then, we heard men screaming their lungs out. These screams came from the girls' village. They were distant but could be heard clearly.

"They are not here!"

"The rascals are not here too!"

"Go towards the mango tree! I want the morons back here right now! Shoot them on their legs the second you spot them, so that they don't have the audacity to run away the next time!"

"Oh no!" The little girl's eyes were welling up. She gripped her sister even more firmly.

"Do you two know how to climb a tree?" Vihaan asked, hurriedly.

"Yes," said the older girl.

"No," replied the younger one, timidly.

"Climb on my back," Vihaan ordered, looking at the younger girl. It was typical of Vihaan to take the initiative, protecting people and caring for them. He didn't bother if his own life was put at stake. Helping the helpless was always his first priority.

"Now, we need to be quick and remain calm. You'll falter if you panic, and we cannot afford that. Okay?" he said sternly but softly.

"Go! We'll manage down here!" I urged.

They started climbing and within thirty seconds or so, were nowhere to be seen. We braced ourselves for the approaching interrogations and threats and were just finalising our plan when five men with bludgeons and guns appeared in front of us. We looked at them innocently, as if ignorant of the two girls we had met, their misery and their precarious situation.

"Hey! Did you see two girls hiding anywhere here?" bellowed one of the men.

"How are we supposed to see them if they are hiding?" Eric counter-questioned.

"For heaven's sake, shut up!" Eva said through gritted teeth to Eric. "I'm sorry. He's slightly sick in the head. Please don't mind him. No, we haven't seen any girl around here."

"Yes, we've been here for the past twenty minutes, roughly, and we've seen no one else come here," I contributed.

"I hope you are not lying?" one of the other men asked.

"No! Why shall we?" I asked defensively.

"I don't know! You might sympathise with and protect your pathetic kind," the former man replied.

"Sir," Eva was on her feet, slowly advancing towards the men. Stopping a few paces in front of them, she said, "We are being extremely respectful and considerate towards people whom we heard hurling abuses and threats to children a few minutes ago. You don't have the right to demean us. It'll be better for all of us if you continue with your hunt and leave us to ourselves," Eva retorted sternly. Eva and her recipient had now entered into a glaring competition, which Eva soon won on account of a fly which decided to rest on the man's eye. It was funny – a huge man fighting a tiny fly. He finally succeeded, gave us a last warning, and took his herd back to the village. When we were certain that they were out of earshot, Eva came back and heaved a sigh of relief. We decided to follow the men for a while to make certain of the safety of the two girls and Vihaan. We came back after a few minutes, satisfied.

"Hey!" Eric called out towards the mango tree.

"Shush! Don't shout! What if they hear us?" Eva warned.

"Stay here and keep guard. I'll bring them down. If anybody comes, yell "hello" to alert us," I instructed.

Fortunately for us, nobody came, and we were able to safely rescue the two girls from the brutes. The second we were on solid ground, the little girl jumped from Vihaan's back and seized her sister, who now seemed much more relieved and much less sceptical of us.

"Let us go behind that bush where you were hiding. Those men might come back, and we need to keep you safe," Eva suggested.

After we had positioned ourselves out of immediate view of the three pathways, the older girl began, "I cannot thank you enough. You risked your lives for two girls whom you had met not an hour back. Thank you so much!" Her eyes were filled with tears of gratitude.

"Of course, we'd risk our lives for children who we know share the same rotten fate as us! Even we run away from our houses when it feels like a frenzied melee there," Eric replied in a matter-of-factly way.

"Exactly. You're completely safe with us," Vihaan said, warmly.

"But what are your names? Tell us about yourselves!" I insisted.

7

ACQUAINTANCE WITH ANOTHER WORLD

"My name is Nazia, and she is my younger sister, Taheera," she said, pointing towards the little girl who was now clutching her sister's frock in her fist. "I'm seven years old and she is five. I've been beaten up numerous times for going against my father and grandfather. See the scar here?" she pointed at the top right corner of her forehead. "My father was thrashing my mother and I tried to intervene by pulling my father by his shirt, and he retaliated by pushing me towards the wall. Even though I banged my head on the wall and was feeling somewhat dizzy, I got up and charged at him again; this time, pushing him away from my mother with a loud grunt. He fell on the floor. But he was not defeated. He got back to his feet, and before I could protect myself, he slapped me so hard, I started bleeding from my ear and the imprint of his big, fat hand stayed for a week. The way I remember that night is that it wasn't my father who had slapped me; it was a monster. He must have yelled at me for two to three minutes – the contents of which I can't recall. I was too busy with my ringing ear and burning cheek. While storming off, he threw his bottle of alcohol at me, deliberately aiming it a few centimetres away from my face. Although the bottle failed to hit me, a shard of the glass failed to miss my forehead. And hence, that night, I got two temporary gifts and one eternal blessing."

Everybody was listening with gaping mouths and incredulous eyes, except me; I was on the brink of tears. The rest of my friends had witnessed such episodes at their houses but had never experienced them. I, on the other hand, had vividly pictured the entire incident as she had narrated, but for a minor replacement – I was the girl with the bleeding ear, burning cheek and scarred face.

"Our father is a bad man. I don't like him." This was the first time that Taheera had spoken. Her voice was a concoction of fear, abhorrence, and a child-like innocence which peaked on these other emotions. She was a small five-year-old girl whose childhood had been brutally throttled in front of her eyes and her mind marred for the rest of her life. "Today was the first time he slapped me when I told him that I wanted to go to school. I had heard Nazia asking my father about going to school a couple of times before, and I had seen the repercussions too. I have always been too afraid to ask my father for anything, but this time, I was stubborn! I yearned to get out of that house and go to a school and study. So, without first discussing this with Nazia – because I knew that she wouldn't let me talk to him – I straightaway went to our father. For the first few seconds, he stared at me blankly. Then, he yelled out Nazia's name."

"'Nazia! Come here, you schmuck!' She came running from the kitchen, but before she could halt, she was slapped across her face and thrown to the floor. 'I know you filled your sister's brain with all this crap of going to school. It has to be you! You've always been the rebellious, shameless imp of this house! This girl (pointing at me) never had the nerve to look me in the eye, and today, she is demanding "education!" I am warning you, you little brat – stop corrupting your sister. Or else…"'

"'Or else what?' Nazia retorted. 'What will you do? You'll hit me, won't you? Then hit me! HIT ME!' And she got slapped once again. His hand's imprint was much darker now. 'That's it? Is that all you can do? You've always slapped me. HIT ME! BEAT ME!' Our father's eyes had never been bigger. Nazia got up and handed him a *laathi*. 'Come on! Beat me with this! Prove your strength! COME ON!'"

"'NO!' our mother yelled. She came in front of Nazia and pleaded with her husband. 'She's just a kid. Please forgive her. I'll talk to her! But please don't hit her with that!'"

"'Move aside! She wants me to hit her, doesn't she? Then, she'll get what she wants. This is her first reasonable demand in the pathetic seven years of her life. She'll get it.' He shoved Ma away so hard that she banged her forehead on the wall. He had raised the *laathi* and was about to bring it down on Nazia when…"

"When Taheera the Superwoman entered the scene!" Nazia exclaimed, throwing her hands up in the air. We started giggling but Taheera's glare to her sister put us in check.

"What? Why are looking at me like that?" Nazia asked, still chuckling.

"Are you making fun of me?" Taheera asked, frowning, standing akimbo.

"NO! How can I make fun of the Superwoman?" Nazia asked mockingly.

"Then it's alright." We exchanged looks and were still giggling when Taheera brought us back to the history of the runaway sisters.

"SO! I stood in front of Nazia with my arms stretched out and screamed, 'NO! You will…' But before I could finish, he had slapped me with the back of his hand and flung me to the floor."

"'You little cockroach! Don't try to be what you aren't! You're just a tiny, filthy cockroach! And cockroaches are supposed to crawl on the ground, not fly in the sky!' He called me filthy and compared me to a COCKROACH!" Taheera's voice slightly cracked as she exclaimed her shock.

"After this, there was no way he could be stopped," Nazia continued. "Has it ever happened to you that you've suppressed your emotions far beyond the limit, and at one point, the burden of these suppressed emotions becomes too heavy to carry, and you assuage your baggage with frantic waves gushing out of your eyes? Well, in our father's case, the baggage was basically anger, frustration, dissatisfaction with two petty daughters, insecurity of power and intimidation by two little girls. He unburdened himself by incessantly and mercilessly thrashing and beating me until our grandfather came and finally put a stop to his fury." She took a pause, regained her breath, and continued, "You think your father will protect you if you ever encounter any danger, but why doesn't it ever occur to anybody that the father might himself be the danger?"

Her monologue had silenced all of us. Our tongues felt heavy, our lips glued together. Our speechlessness was not because of shock or incredulity, but because this was the first time someone had abbreviated our own lives with perfect precision. The silence that ensued for the next two to three minutes witnessed emotions ranging from realisation and familiarity to sympathy and agitation.

Finally breaking the silence, Eva asked in a hushed tone, "So, how did you reach here in the bushes?"

"When our grandfather arrived and told our father to stop being a lunatic, he announced that he intended to stop only after putting an end to my demands and rebellions forever. He wanted to kill me." One can expect this revelation to evoke nervous gasps from the rest of us, but it didn't. It seemed natural.

"I got up slowly and painfully, took hold of my sister while our father and grandfather were still arguing, and jumped out of the window. And we ran. We ran as if they had let loose a hundred tigers behind us and we had to run for our lives. This was our last chance. Either we run and live, or we turn around and die. So, we ran as fast as Taheera's small legs and my bruised legs could take us."

"Hey! My legs are not small," Taheera admonished Nazia.

"They are, just like your brain and your entire body. Now keep shut." Taheera was still scowling at Nazia as she continued, "We finally lost track of them and reached this place outside our village, where the bushes were large enough to hide both of us. We didn't dare budge, in case those men saw us. Instead, we met you!"

8

DADU

"Well, we have to think ahead now," Vihaan said. "They can't go back to that prison where they'll be guillotined the second someone sets eyes upon them."

"Wow! Someone has been reading about the French Revolution," Eric remarked, nudging Vihaan on the elbow with a playful grin. "But if they can't go back to their house, where else will they go?" asked Eric.

"Do you think Dadu will help us?" I proposed.

Dadu was an incredibly old man who owned a small ration shop – our second favourite rendezvous after the mango tree – on the outskirts of the three villages, a few steps away from the common river. In this shop, he ate, slept, worked and lived. This river was a demarcation between the earth's embellishments and the worms squirming through the grimy earth; the sky-soaring buildings and the barely existing mud huts; the sophisticated and the destitute. Nobody was ever allowed to cross that river. But we could bathe in the river water and play and swim around to our heart's content. After a long, wet summer morning, we would go to Dadu and he would give us little toffees of different flavours free of cost. This was a secret because no one else in the village was worthy enough of this privilege.

Dadu's frame could hardly support him for more than a few minutes. Always clothed in white, there was no other colour we could possibly imagine him in. His tiny face was a field of running wrinkles, but he had the most vivacious laugh one could ever hear in their lifetime. It could awaken the dead, enliven the most dejected, enthuse the mundane flowing water and rhapsodise the monotony of the fluttering birds. Being the father figure of the entire village, he'd be as attentive to our relentless, animated jabber as concerned about our violent lives. God too was probably very eager to meet him.

"I don't think we have any other option. Let's take them to him. We'll see what happens," Eva replied. "Come with us," Eva motioned to Nazia and Taheera.

There were narrow pathways between each village which ultimately led to the river. They were walled on either side by tall wheat stocks or paddy stocks all through the year. We went through the one between my village and Eric and Eva's. These pathways were so slender that nobody could ever use them for grazing or walking their animals. As a result, they were as even as paper with small pebbles lying hither and thither and we had to walk in a single file to fit in. It was almost dark. We had to be extremely cautious and absolutely inaudible so as to not alert anybody nearby.

"Nazia," Taheera called, whispering.

"Yes?" Nazia replied, whispering too.

"Do you think Ma saw us?"

"When? While we were escaping?"

"Yes."

"Oh, yes. She definitely saw us."

"Why do you think she didn't stop us?"

"Because she doesn't want to ruin her daughters' lives the way her parents ruined hers. She knows that she's helpless, but her daughters aren't."

I couldn't help but overhear this brief *tete-a-tete*. At that age, I could not fathom the amount of love she had for her own children and the magnitude of malaise for her own life. She sacrificed her daughters to protect them from the torment she was condemned to live in for perpetuity; even if it meant never seeing them again or caressing their hair or singing lullabies to them or applying ointment after an episode of wrath by their father or in the least, hugging them ever again.

"Hello! There are my favourite children again!" Dadu's voice echoed through the stillness. "And I see they've brought company this time! But why is this company so wounded?"

"Hello, Dadu!" We chorused and embraced him tightly, except Taheera and Nazia. He kissed us individually on our foreheads before letting go of us.

"Dadu, they are sisters – Taheera and Nazia (pointing at them separately)," said Eva. "They are from the village farthest away from here."

"We need your help," interjected Eric.

"You'll get all the help you need, Eric. But first, let's tend to their wounds. Why didn't you take them to the hospital?"

"Because they've run away," Vihaan replied.

"And can't be seen," Eric added.

We gave him the entire account of their abusive household, ruthless father, helpless mother, involuntarily complicit grandparents, the mammoth escape, our discovery, the brief but dire assemblage below the tree and the ultimate conjecture of Dadu being our only resort.

"Okay. But the girls are bleeding. What do we do about that?" asked Dadu.

"Do you not have something in your shop?" I asked.

"*Hmm*, I do have some sanitiser and cotton. But I'm not sure if they'll be helpful. What if the wounds are too deep?"

"I don't think they are. I know how deeper wounds feel," Nazia replied with a straight face.

Dadu stared at her for a few seconds before saying, "Okay, then. Come here both of you." With utmost care, and very meticulously, he cleaned their wounds. Taheera shrieked each time the cotton touched her wound. But Nazia was more controlled; even though the pain was visible on her face, she did not make it evident. All of us were silent when Dadu was tending to them, trying to ensure that he was not disturbed and offering help whenever needed.

Once he was done, Eva asked, "We were wondering if they could stay with you in your shop?"

"Sure, they can. But what if some customer sees them and reports it to their father? They are not safe here."

"Yes…We didn't think of that…," I said with a discouraged face.

"Have you thought of any other place where they can hide?" Dadu had sensed our eagerness to help them out, and how helpless we were feeling.

"No."

"Well, what about the storeroom in your school? It's been locked for ages. Anybody hardly ever goes to that room. I don't remember the last time that room got any fresh air or sunlight. That might be a nice hideout for them. We'll supply them with food and blankets, and you can come and play with them outside when no one's watching. I'll keep guard."

"Yes!" exclaimed Eric. "Dadu, that's an amazing idea!"

"Yes, Dadu! We love you so much!" added Vihaan and we hugged him tightly.

"And I love all of you!" Dadu replied lovingly.

After we had released him, Nazia stepped forward and said, "Thank you so much, Dadu. You've saved our lives, and I can't thank you enough for it."

"Don't worry, my dear. They are all my children. So, their friends too are my children. Think of me as your father. Whenever you need me, I'll always be there."

"No! We can't think of you as our father! Our father is a monster! You're an angel," Taheera said and ran to him, cuddling him with her tiny arms. Dadu laughed and kissed her on her forehead. He stretched his left arm towards Nazia, who, though hesitantly, went to him and hugged him. Finally, Nazia and Taheera had found a home.

9

A ROSE AND A SECRET

The following dawn brought with it four children and one old man, who had vowed to make this world a more sufferable place to live in. I woke up to the sun gently kissing my eyes and an unusual peace in the house. I looked at our ancient wall clock which soon explained the unusual peace. It was 4:45 a.m. and the entire village was still in deep slumber. The four of us had decided to meet Dadu by 5:00 the previous evening. A long day awaited us, and we didn't want to dawdle.

I got out through my usual escape route but was instantly stopped in my tracks.

"Tamanna! Wait!" It was Durga Di. "Where are you going so early in the morning?"

"I am meeting my friends at Dadu's. We have some important business," I said calmly. I knew Durga Di would never tell on me, and my secret would be safe with her.

"Important business, huh? And what exactly is that, may I know?"

"Of course, you may! But you have to promise to never utter a word about this to anyone," I said sternly as if I were the big sister.

"Yes, I promise."

"We've made new friends."

"So? Isn't that a good thing?"

"Not if you know *how*."

"Well, I *want* to know."

"They are from the third village." At this, her face grew sombre. "And they ran away from their house yesterday."

"What?" She literally yelled in a whisper.

"Yes. They are two sisters. The elder one, Nazia, is my age, and the younger one, Taheera, is five. All of us know for a fact that we have very similar families. So, we could not let them go back. They might have been killed."

"Killed? What do you mean 'killed?'"

"Taheera asked their father if they could go to school. He got infuriated because until now, it was only Nazia who had demanded education. Taheera didn't dare look at her father in the eyes. So, he inferred that Nazia put this idea into Taheera's head. He slapped Nazia, beat her mercilessly with a lathi, and had intended to kill her when their grandfather intervened. The father and son got busy arguing, which gave Nazia and Taheera the opportunity to sneak out. We found them hiding behind a bush near the mango tree."

"Oh dear," Durga Di gasped. "So, what are your plans now? Where will they stay?"

"We took them to Dadu. They spent the night at his place, but we've decided to make the storeroom in our school habitable for them. Nobody ever enters that room. Even Dadu said that it'd be safe for them."

"So, that's why you're going there now?"

"Yes."

"Well, I can't say that you're not risking your lives for these two girls, but I don't see any other option either." She gave me a smile which conveyed emotions words will be ever incapable of. "Now run! You're already late! And don't worry; I'll cover for you. You have my full support in this. Tell me if you need anything. Okay?"

"Okay!" I was already on my heels when I turned around and said, "Di!"

"Yes?" I dashed towards her and hugged her like a baby monkey clinging to its mother.

"I love you so much," I said with faintly wet eyes.

"I know," she said softly and kissed me on my head. "Now, don't start crying! Run away!" And I hastened with rapid strides towards Dadu's shop.

Since it was a Sunday, our school was closed, which proved to be both favourable as well as unfavourable to us. It was favourable because we could carry out our mission with complete discretion, and unfavourable because the door was locked. But living in abusive families had its advantages too – we never knew what it meant to be defeated.

"Don't worry. Leave it to me," Eva assured. She took a hairpin out of her hair, crouched down, inserted the pin into the lock, and put her left ear near the lock to listen to its "heart-beat," as she called it.

"So, our Miss Proper can be naughty too, huh?" I teased.

"I didn't know you could do that!" Eric exclaimed.

"I have many hidden talents, Eric."

"Being a thief might be one of them," mocked Vihaan.

"*Ha ha.* Funny. Now, try shutting up and let me concentrate."

Click! Eva had opened the lock!

"For the first time, I am proud of you, sister," Eric said, patting Eva on her shoulder.

"Thank you, Eric. I wish I could say that too." It wasn't Eva's retort which cracked us up as much as Eric's vanquished expression.

"Come on! Don't make that face," she said playfully and pulled Eric's arm and all of us went inside. We went straight and as we passed by the empty corridor, I peeked inside one of the sections of class 7. My head went topsy-turvy when I saw what was written on the board – 20a+10=70, 15x-5=55. '*Why are there English alphabets with numbers?*' I remember thinking. The storeroom was at the end of that long corridor. We tread very lightly because we were in the midst of absolute silence, and we didn't want to alert even the tiniest dirt particle.

Eva repeated the demonstration of her hidden talent once again when we reached the storeroom. On opening the door, we were met with a cloud of dust which blew past us like a spectre. The next few minutes had us coughing as if we had inhaled the smoke from a chimney. After we had recollected ourselves and had made certain that Dadu wasn't particularly distressed, we entered the storeroom.

"Woah! This is going to be much more difficult than I'd credited it for," said Eric, standing akimbo.

"Why? Did you think that a room which hadn't been opened for ages would have transformed into a palace by now?" I asked.

"Whatever, at least I hadn't expected it to be so bad."

"You should start expecting less," said Eva. "Come on. We need to get to work now!"

The three hours that followed involved rapid sweeping, fervent mopping and extremely tedious dusting. The cobwebs and cockroaches in each nook and corner only added to our task, with frequent shrieks from Taheera as she saw a spider sleeping in its web or an agitated cockroach scurrying away to seek shelter after being revealed. We brought spare mattresses, sheets and pillows from Dadu's house, which were initially owned by his late wife. We arranged the chairs which were strewn about in a disorderly fashion prior to our readjustments. The useless items, occupying unnecessary space in the room, were tossed inside the cupboard. We inserted a branch inside the handles to prevent it from opening and unleashing a load of garbage.

"Wow! We *are* talented people, aren't we?" Eric asked, his face red with perspiration and adrenaline.

"I hate to say this, but I agree with you," replied Vihaan. "We've done a pretty good job, I guess?"

"All of you have done an amazing job!" exclaimed Dadu. "And I'm so proud of you for helping your new friends whom you had not met before yesterday."

"Yes. We truly are grateful," chimed in Nazia. "Thank you so much!"

"Shut up. We might not know what a "family" means, but we are well aware of the role friendship plays in our lives," said Eva.

"Yes, and we'd do anything for you since we are friends now," I said.

"And you all can become one big family!" said Dadu.

"But isn't a family related by blood?" asked Taheera.

"Not necessarily. On one hand, we have a family we are born into, and on the other hand, we have a family which we choose for ourselves as life goes on. The latter family is our friends – people whom we live for, and if need be, will die for. So, always cherish your friendship with each other and you'll eventually understand what a family means," said Dadu. "Can I get a group hug now?" And he got one.

"*Kabaddi kabaddi kabaddi kabaddi....*" Eric could be heard saying under his breath that he was the first raider. We were playing *kabaddi* and the teams were divided such that Eva, Eric and I were in one team, and Nazia and Vihaan in the other since Vihaan was a strong contender and we were still unaware of Nazia's skills. Taheera was our referee and Dadu our audience. We had made the storeroom acceptable and had some chips and juice for breakfast from Dadu's shop. Luckily, Dadu hadn't had any customers until then, nor had we seen any children or women approach the river to bathe or wash their clothes.

"You won't be able to hold me for long," Eric told Nazia with a mocking smile, who was in the opposite team.

"We'll see that," Nazia replied with a lopsided grin.

Instantaneously, Eric tagged Nazia, who pulled both his legs, causing him to fall down on his stomach. She pulled him further backwards, creating a safe distance between him and the mid-line. She proceeded to throw herself on top of him, clutched him by his torso and wrapped his legs with her own to prevent him from wriggling like a puppy.

"One, two, three, four, five, six, seven, eight, nine, ten! And he's out!" exclaimed Taheera.

"Wow! What do you eat?" Eric asked, puffing with loss of breath and brushing his shirt and shorts.

"Definitely less than what you eat. I can assure you," Nazia replied, grinning.

"Then where do you get all that strength from?"

"God's gift, I guess," replied Nazia, shrugging. "I hope you haven't broken any ribs. You seem so dainty and fragile," Nazia said with feigned concern, her eyes glistening with mischief.

"Hey! I'm neither dainty nor fragile! You're just abnormally strong!" Eric retorted.

"Just accept it, Eric. You've been *defeated*," teased Vihaan.

Eric blessed Vihaan with his typical glare which never failed to tickle our stomachs. We burst out laughing and Eric walked off declaring he didn't intend to play anymore.

"Children! Get inside the school right now! I think I heard some rustling near the crops," cautioned Dadu in a hushed voice. We immediately ran inside the school, closed the door and darted straight to the storeroom. We could see from the window just opposite the storeroom in the corridor that they were the very same men who had been searching for Nazia and Taheera the previous day. It seemed as if they were interrogating Dadu because Dadu would have been rummaging through his products had they been mere customers.

"We'll have to lock the room from outside!" Eric cried out.

"But that'd mean that the person who locks will stay outside!" pointed out Taheera.

"It's alright. I'll lock the door and go and hide in the girls' washroom," I offered.

"Tamanna, are you sure?" asked Eva.

"Yes, of course! We don't have any other option, do we?" I replied.

"I'll go instead of you!" intervened Vihaan.

"What difference will it make? Moreover, I am better at hide and seek than any of you," I said with a wink. "Don't worry about me. I'll be fine." All this while we had crouched below the window to avoid getting our throats slit. "Now get inside so I can lock it."

After reassuring myself that I had fastened the door securely and that the lock was intact, I scampered towards the girls' washroom, which was mid-way through the second corridor after taking a left. I went inside the washroom and hid in one of the cubicles. I was waiting with bated breath and had begun to wonder if Dadu was safe, and if the men had gone when I heard muffled voices outside the washroom.

"Check inside this washroom," I heard someone command.

Instinctively, I stood on one leg on the tap beside the toilet, put my other leg in a small hole which some blessed kid might have dug to save me unwittingly on that precarious day, pulled myself up to the window perpendicular to the toilet with all the strength I could muster, and jumped out of it. The dry grass below my feet created a slight noise which alerted the men inside. By the time they deciphered where the noise had come from, I had already run away to the adjacent side of the building, headed towards the wilderness just opposite our school and hid behind a large bush.

I was panting violently and had to put my hand on my mouth to muffle my frenzied breath. After regaining control of my breath, I tried to look towards the school. I supported myself on my left hand and left knee and was about to further bend to my left when I felt a sharp pang surge through my entire leg. I wedged my clenched fist inside my mouth to stifle my groan. Retreating to my normal position, I realised what had caused that pang of pain – the stem of a rose plant. It had adorned my left knee with countless tiny thorns. Added to the beauty was blood spurting out of the little interstices. I longed to stretch out my leg, but I couldn't do that without disturbing the nearby shrubs and bushes and attracting the attention of those ghastly men because of whom I had to torture myself with that excruciating throbbing in my knee.

With every passing second, the pain climbed higher levels of anguish, rendering it difficult to inhibit the burst of tears and the cries of agony. I tried regaining my composure after a couple of minutes and removed my hand from my mouth. Pressing my lips against each other, lest a groan should escape my mouth, I proceeded to remove the thorns. As I removed the first thorn, it proved my prudence in pressing my lips together. It was as tiny as the agony was mammoth. Soaked in my blood, I put it down beside me with quivering hands. Had I continued at this rate, I would have severely bruised both my lips before removing all the thorns. I calmed myself, loosened my lips slightly, and was about to continue when I heard a call.

"Tamanna! Where are you?" It was Eric's voice.

My brief tryst with the rose stem had made me forget all about the men, Dadu and my friends. I was so fixated on not letting a cry break free that I had completely forgotten the reason behind this restraint.

"Tamanna! You can come out now! The men have gone." I recognised it to be Vihaan's voice. He was close.

Still crouching, I held myself on my right knee and peeked behind the bush to scan the area for any camouflaged danger.

"I'm here!" I waved my hand at Vihaan and flopped back on the ground. I was feeling an overwhelming urge to chop off my leg with each passing second. Being only seven years old, I had never thought that I'd be compelled to question the nature of such a contentious creation – a rose. *What is the point of its being so beautiful when it is capable of causing piercing agony at even the slightest touch?*

I was in tears by the time Vihaan found me.

"Tamanna! Are you…" He stopped mid-sentence when he saw my knee.

"Bloody hell!" he exclaimed, his voice gradually rising to a crescendo.

"Hey! Where did you learn that from?" I asked, scowling at him.

"Are you in your senses? Or have these thorns pricked your brain too? Your knee is bleeding like a waterfall and all you care about is where I learnt a petty slang from?" he reproached.

"Well, that's not 'all' I care about," I said in a manner when a small child had been admonished by her mother.

"Oh really? For your information Tamanna, we live in a village, and not in a posh British estate where people faint at even the mention of a slang."

"Okay, there's no need to scold me like that," I told him in a half-hurt, half-relieved tone. Relieved, because I knew that there was someone who cared about me. It was one of those moments that comes out of nowhere – a realisation that dawns on you when you least expect it to.

"Will you care to tell me how on Earth this happened?" By this time, our entire party had gathered around us upon hearing Vihaan yell.

"Holy shit! What the hell happened?" This time, it was Eva. I looked at her dumbstruck. Our Miss Proper not only knew how to open locks with a hairpin but slang too!

"It was the rose," I said, pointing towards it.

"We'll have to take her to the hospital!" Eric interjected.

"But what about Nazia and Taheera?" I asked.

"Tamanna, please, you've already done a lot for us; all of you. I'm not really sure right now whether I'm more grateful or regretful of meeting you in the first place," Nazia replied with a solemn face. "You should all take her to the hospital. Taheera and I will be here. Don't worry about us."

Vihaan and Eric took me by the shoulders and lifted me up cautiously. Our journey from one end of the planet to the other can be described as nothing but painful. Added to my physical agony, was the mental affliction of being wary of those awful men.

We reached the hospital after an eternity and our strangely propitious fate allowed us to do so safely. Our village hospital could be called a dilapidated ruin by a city-dweller or anyone who viewed it from miles away, although it wouldn't be wrong to mention that it was a much better ruin than the other hospitals in the vicinity. It had a three-storey building for conducting surgeries and for patients who needed prolonged treatment and hence, required to be admitted, and a cube-shaped clinic beside it for treating minor ailments. I dare say we had high-end, sophisticated doctors and nurses, for the doctors were just men who had studied medicine and received their medical degree from the local college, and the nurses were old widows who had nobody else to sustain but themselves, and so, devoted their lives in the healing of the ill.

Striking apart from the spurious amateurs was Dr Adam. He was a good-humoured, educated man, who was the village's general physician and had received his medical degree from Harvard Medical School, USA. Despite belonging to an inter-religious and dysfunctional family, he didn't let the iron chains of his troubled past and present impair him from dreaming of his own future and succeeded at materialising it too. He was a general physician, but his knowledge of Western medicine, diagnoses and treatments of the most unimaginable diseases bestowed him with the sobriquet "The Wisest Man on Earth." His office was the clinic where we were headed to.

"Can we see the doctor, please?" Eva asked the receptionist in a hurried tone.

"Let me see if he is available. Why don't you sit there while I check on him?" She was a kind lady.

"Oh, no! I won't be able to get up after that. Please hurry up!" I replied.

"Yes, yes."

The doctor met us with a beaming smile upon entering his chamber, revealing a jesting glisten and a genuinely concerned twinkle in his eyes.

"Well, how may I help you today?" he asked in a pleasantly soothing voice.

"Do you not have eyes of your own? Can't you see?" Eric yelled back at him.

"I swear to God, if you don't shut up, you won't be returning home today with your own pair of eyes," Eva threatened Eric through gritted teeth. She turned towards the doctor and said, "I'm really sorry for his rudeness. He's my brother, although I don't know why or how (she said this in a hushed tone while glaring at Eric). All four of us were playing and she – Tamanna – fell on a rose stem. Do you think the thorns are dangerous?"

"Well, if you hadn't brought her to me, then the thorns might have proven to be pretty dangerous. But since you're here now, you need not worry." He had still not lost his smile.

He took out the thorns – eight in all - with his tweezers and then applied some antiseptic liquid to prevent any infection. Thankfully, the thorns weren't buried in my skin too deep, so it didn't hurt as much, but the antiseptic definitely burned. He ended the procedure by bandaging my knee after putting an ointment over the wounds. He handed me an unused tube of that ointment and a fresh roll of the bandage and instructed me to change the dressing once every day after my bath.

"But I don't have any money, neither to pay you nor for these," I said with a sullen face.

"It's alright. I don't charge children for having fun." He winked at me playfully and gave that same beaming smile with which he had welcomed us. "Take care. You should all go home now. It's getting dark."

"Thank you so much," I said, and we left his clinic.

"I'll escort Tamanna to her house. Why don't you go and inform Dadu that everything went fine?" Eva told the boys.

"Okay. Wait for me near the mango tree," replied Eric.

"Okay."

"Come on," Vihaan pulled Eric by his sleeves, and they ran away.

"Nazia seemed upset earlier today, didn't she?" I asked Eva. We had entered my village and were headed towards my house.

"She did seem quite disturbed to me," Eva replied.

"Do you think it was out of fear of the men or concern for me?"

"I think a more suitable combination would be *regret* and concern."

"Do you know what I realised today?"

"What?"

"I always thought of the rose as the most beautiful flower. You give your partner a rose while proposing to them as a symbol of love, a symbol of eternity. Even during weddings, people decorate the place with roses. You gift someone a rose and their face instantly lights up. The rose carries so much meaning. Always. But today, I spent the entire day cursing roses. I kept muttering to myself that they are so horrible, why are people so fond of roses, they are so thorny, etc. But now I realise that even friendships are like roses."

"How so?"

"Because even they are not always peaceful. They are not all rosy and fragrant and hunky-dory. Sometimes there are 'ups', and some other times there are 'downs'. For instance, today was a 'down'. But that doesn't mean that it's a bad friendship. Just like the thorns don't make the flower 'bad'. Despite knowing that its thorns can hurt them, people still love the flower. When we love someone – when we commit ourselves to them – we put ourselves in a risky position, a position where we might get hurt. So, do we stop loving? Do we stop making friends? No. We just learn to accept the hurt. We learn to deal with it; because the beauty of that relationship, that friendship, that love, is much more than the pain or hurt."

"So, the rose isn't an entirely horrible flower, right?" Eva asked with a smile.

"Right," I replied, returning her smile.

I was still a few paces away from my house when I said goodbye to her. I couldn't risk bringing her near my family. They already disapproved of my friendships; bringing a "different" friend near the house would have proven scandalous.

"Good night, Tamanna. I'm sure Durga Di will take care of you," said Eva, smiling.

"Yes, she is the only person who knows that word in the house," I replied mockingly. "I'll see you tomorrow at Dadu's."

"Yes, we'll have to check on Nazia and Taheera too."

"That is precisely why. Good night."

As I turned around, my eldest brother caught my eye. He had been spying on me from the gateway. He averted his eyes and went inside the house the second he saw me. I understood what was in store for me. Yet, I didn't run away and limped along. I hadn't had the fortune of even closing the door properly when the bombardment commenced.

"Where were you the whole day?" Ma inquired.

"Rahul says that he saw you with that girl again," said my grandmother.

"Why did you leave the house without informing anyone?" This particular question came to me as a shock since it was delivered by my unusually present father.

"Oh, God! What happened to your leg? Are you okay?" It need not be mentioned who cared to look at my leg.

"I'll answer all your questions," I replied, firmly.

"Well, come here and sit first!" Again, the interjection is self-explanatory.

"Sure! She *is* the daughter of the landlady, isn't she?" remarked my grandmother.

"Don't worry. I won't sit until I've satisfied all your doubts," I said with an outward confidence that didn't exactly comply with the inward repugnance.

"I was with Dadu the whole day and then at the hospital," I said looking at Ma. I swerved towards my grandmother and said, "Yes, what he said is right. We were together the whole day. She supported me all the way here, as you can very well see, I have hurt my knee." I swivelled to my right to face my father and said, "Wow!

You're surprisingly here. Isn't it amazing how I cause much less trouble by staying away from this house, than you by staying *in* it?" I had seen Ma's burned hand and bleeding forehead which she so artfully tried to conceal. "To answer your question; I didn't feel it necessary," I said with a shrug.

"What do you mean "you didn't feel it necessary" you dirty little moth?" he growled with a menacingly disgusted face.

"I mean what you understand. I would have informed somebody if I felt anybody would care," I replied matter-of-factly.

"Do you mean, you didn't even inform Durga Di?" asked Naveen.

"Which world do you live in, Naveen? Did I not, in front of you, tell Ma that she had woken up early and gone to Dadu's to help him in his shop?" said Durga Di.

"I was present there too, but I thought you had just made that up," commented Rahul.

"Oh! So, you can think too? You're capable of that?" I mocked.

This question was received by a steel glass hurled at me, which I scarcely missed. "How dare you talk to your elder brother in that manner?" It was, of course, my grandmother.

"Because…" I began.

"Tamanna!" Ma intruded. "Let's give it a rest for today. Wash up and I'll give you dinner."

"No. She won't get any dinner today. Let her sleep hungry. That should teach her how to talk to her brothers and elders." The verdict was given, and the court adjourned. The judge then closed in on me and muttered with clenched teeth, "The day I find out about your little secrets, you'll wish you were never born."

"Don't worry about that. I wish that every day, especially when I'm inside this house," I replied, returning his glare.

I didn't sleep on an empty stomach that night. While serving, Durga Di kept some *dal* aside for me and Ma purposely baked some extra chapattis which she passed off as an innocent mistake. When the jungle was silent and the animals were all in deep slumber, Ma said, "I know you were up to something today. I want to know *what*."

"It's a secret, Ma. Good night." I gave her a tender kiss on her forehead from where she was previously bleeding and drifted away. That day, I realised that some secrets are supposed to be treasured even more than your life, especially when these secrets start inhabiting a cosy niche in your heart.

10

BATTLE WITH ONESELF

It was a lovely day. The sun shone amiably, greeting us with an invigorating warmth on a cool, autumn morning. The birds could be heard chittering in the trees or fluttering away in their frivolous games. The wind blew, singing soft, low melodies in our ears and shrouding our faces in its tenderness. The mountains were a rocky phantom because of the light haze fast approaching us. The village was still traversing its dreams when I woke up and escaped through my usual escape route. It had been a couple of months since the game of hide and seek with those "men", and the days which followed thus were as humdrum as taking a walk in a park full of predators. Out of habit, I went to the well, washed my face and headed towards the mango tree. Expectedly or unexpectedly, I found Eric and Eva there.

"Good morning!" I greeted. "What are you two doing here?"

"We could ask you the same question, and I'm sure our answers won't differ," replied Eric. We gave each other wry smiles, finding solace in the familiarity of our situations.

"I guess Vihaan's having the time of his life with his family," said Eva.

"I wouldn't say so. There have been talks of Durga Di and Rihan Bhaiya's marriage, which haven't been entirely peaceful," I said.

"What do you mean?" asked Eva and Eric together.

"Rihan Bhaiya and Durga Di don't want the marriage, but our families are adamant about it."

"Why doesn't Rihan Bhaiya want to marry Durga Di?" asked Eric.

"Because he thinks she is too young, and moreover, he knows she doesn't want to marry him."

"So, basically, Rihan Bhaiya considers Durga Di a human being," said Eva.

"Yes."

There was a pause; not an awkward one, but one which lingers on after a peculiar revelation. It was nearly impossible for us to process the fact there existed someone who didn't perceive the female race as a *species* consisting only of dimwits.

"Shall we go and meet Nazia and Taheera? They might be up by now," proposed Eva.

"What about Vihaan? What if he comes here and doesn't find us?" asked Eric.

"Then he'll know to look for us at Dadu's," I said.

"Do you think he's alright?" asked Eva, while on our amble to the school.

"Who?" I asked.

"Vihaan," she said.

"Why wouldn't he be?" asked Eric.

"I don't know. It's not usual for him to stay at his house for so long in the morning."

"Good point," I seconded.

"Probably he slept late yesterday, or was just tired," suggested Eric.

"Do you think his mother will let him sleep for so long, whatever be the reason?" I asked rhetorically.

"I think you are worrying unnecessarily; typical girl stuff," he replied.

"Well, if you're implying that girls are more thoughtful than boys, then we'll take that as a compliment," said Eva.

"That's not what I…," started Eric.

"Eric, you don't want to continue this conversation," I said with a warning glare. He rolled his eyes at us and continued walking, sulking.

When we reached Dadu's, we found Nazia and Taheera at his shop, chatting away with him. Dadu and Nazia were arranging the shop, while Taheera sat, enjoining them as if it were a play where she was the boss and Dadu and Nazia her helpless servants.

"Good morning! I see Taheera has found a job for herself!" cried Eva excitedly as she went and hugged Taheera around the neck, who reciprocated with equal ardour.

"Oh, no! She always had one – of eating people's heads and relishing the meal too!" mocked Nazia.

"I think she is pretty good at it," commented Eric.

"Good? She is the best!" exclaimed Nazia. "Aren't you, Taheera?" she asked with a mischievous smile. The scowl and the angry huffs that followed received guffaws from the trees, the river, and us alike. Nature was with us in our happiness.

"Where is Vihaan today?" enquired Nazia.

"Yes! I miss him! He usually takes my side," said Taheera innocently.

"I have no idea," I replied.

"Not a clue," said Eric.

"Shall we go and check at his house?" suggested Eva.

"Can Nazia and I come too?" Taheera asked.

"No. It won't be safe. Why don't you two stay here? If everything's fine, we'll return with Vihaan, and if there's any trouble, one of us will run back and update you," I advised.

"Okay," chorused Nazia and Taheera.

As we directed our steps towards Vihaan's house, we were startled by the magic that morning had ushered.

There were 'different' women, huddled together, exchanging bangles, scarves and sandals, apologising for one missing bangle which must have met its fate by piercing into the wrist which borne it, and without once alluding to the previous night's blighted sandals they were now passing on to another household; there were 'different' men scrutinising the modern agricultural methods, grumbling about pests in their fields and rodents in their storehouses, while manifesting termites in their tongues, and discussing the past night's libido which had resulted in sexual satisfaction for one and conjugal abhorrence for the other; there were older 'different' women babbling animatedly about how their sons were once again successful in their show of innate virility, and how grateful they were for being blessed with goats and cows for daughters-in-law and steal-hearted, empty-headed brutes for sons. There were older 'different' men lamenting about the increasing debts and equally decreasing wages, the ruthlessness of the supposedly revered landlord – the exorbitant rates of interest and inhuman working hours – and the consequential threats of buying the females of the house for compensation. These were some of the topics which united these 'different' people and allied us 'different' children against them.

Finally, we reached Vihaan's house, and the sight that greeted us, could not have been imagined even in the wildest of dreams. His door was bolted. We tried to peek in through the windows, which were, through grilled, not closed. The curtains easily gave way, and we were met with a house in utmost disarray. The furniture – whatever little they had – lay astray, facing whichever direction it pleased; the kitchen utensils were anywhere but in the kitchen; but what grabbed our attention, gradually but fixedly, was a blot of blood on the edge of one of the walls. As we were trying to discern the cause behind that mayhem, a terror crept into our minds – '*What if Vihaan is injured?*' Without diving into any immediate speculation, we decided to ask their neighbour about the proceedings of that morning.

"Oh, it was so horrible! There was screaming, banging, wailing and shouting. This is what we had to wake up to today morning. They were so engrossed in their row that they must have forgotten that it was their *house* and not a battlefield. God! It was so bad; terribly bad. I feel so bad for that poor little boy! He is such a dear soul!" This was the narrative of a plump and dwarfish but sturdy-looking lady who had responded to our desperate, clamorous knocks.

"Wait! Little boy? Are you talking of Vihaan?" I asked, concerned.

"Yes, yes! He is your buddy, isn't he? I've seen you all playing together."

"What happened to him?" we yelled in one voice.

"Well, as I told you, there was a lot of yelling and arguing going on and I could hear metal objects hurled across and creaking of furniture and they were all screaming at the top of their voices…"

"COME TO THE POINT!" She took back a step as I became outraged, furious with her useless and pointless gibber.

"Just answer the question! What happened to Vihaan?" urged Eric impatiently.

"I…I…Uh…," she stuttered, clearly scared of three seven-year-olds. "The yelling suddenly stopped when I heard someone cry out in pain. I came running out of my house to check if everyone was okay and I saw the older boy, Rihan, carrying his brother in his arms, with blood dripping down from his forehead. Their father and mother were close too. They went out of the village, probably to the hospital."

"Was Vihaan conscious?" Eva asked.

"What?" The woman asked with a bewildered face as if the question was too complicated to be comprehended.

"Were his eyes open or closed? Was he making any movement?" elaborated Eva.

"Who? Vihaan?"

"Oh, no, no! *Kumbhkaran*! Remember him? *Raavan's* brother in *Ramayana*. We've been discussing *him* for the past ten minutes, haven't we?" Eric taunted. She looked at him with tears welling up in her eyes, like a three-year-old child who had just been reproached for being naughty.

"Obviously Vihaan! Are you always so dumb?" I scorned.

"Ma'am," Eva urged holding her hand and asking in her calming voice, "Vihaan is our friend and it's crucial for us to know if he is alright. Please tell me whether he was awake when his brother rushed out of the house, or was he sleeping?"

"He must be sleeping," she returned in a choked voice, "because his eyes were closed, and he wasn't saying anything."

"Okay, thank you so much. I'm sorry if we have caused you any discomfort," said Eva.

"Discomfort? *She* was the discomfort – to our minds, our souls and our patience!" said Eric when we had left her house and were heading towards the hospital.

"I had expected *some* gratitude for maintaining my equanimity and not creating a scene," she replied rhetorically.

"*Equa...* what? What did you say?" Eric asked, perplexed.

"Don't blame us for losing our temper! She was acting dumb! Or probably she *is* dumb," I defended.

"Your yelling and taunts didn't really help, did they, except make a poor, old woman cry?"

"*Dumb* and old is more like it," Eric corrected, muttering in my ears.

"Forget about it! I'm worried about Vihaan. I hope he hasn't got a concussion," said Eva.

"Con...con...what?" asked Eric, confused.

"Concussion. It's like a temporary damage to the functioning of the brain. It happens when the head is hit against something solid," I explained.

"Is it dangerous?" asked Eric, scared.

"Depends upon the severity of the injury and the quality of treatment," replied Eva.

"Quality of treatment? How are we going to get *quality* treatment in this damned village?" asked Eric.

"Calm down," I said. "We still have Dr Adam."

"Oh, yes," said Eric, although outwardly satisfied, but visibly still dubious.

Upon entering the gates, we decided to approach Dr Adam first. Our minds felt heavy with fear and worry. The persistent *what if* was too cumbersome. This was a novel feeling for me. I had never felt so anxious for anybody before. I could not fathom it that day, but it was the second time I had been brushed with another nuance of friendship.

"He isn't here, darlings. He is entertaining your friend right now in the hospital," returned the receptionist when questioned about Vihaan. "He's been with him since the past hour. The boy was injured pretty badly, you see," she elaborated in a sympathetic tone.

"Do you know the exact details of what happened to him?" asked Eva.

"No, dear. I'm sorry I can't help you with that," replied the receptionist.

"It's okay. Thank you very much," I said and we exited the clinic.

"We'll have to talk to the hospital receptionist now," I whispered nervously, standing a few paces outside the hospital and aware of the guard's intent eyes on us.

"I don't like her face," remarked Eric, staring at whatever portion of her face was visible from our end.

"She doesn't seem as hospitable as the clinic receptionist," observed Eva.

"Ironic, isn't it?" I said. "Let's go in now."

We entered the hospital and went towards the receptionist with slow, apprehensive steps. We had composed ourselves for the imminent sneers and jibes. One wrong foot, and we were sure to be thrown out of the hospital. While Eric had an uncontrollable and biting tongue, I had a tongue which could flow like lava once my temper erupted. The two of us, therefore, had vowed to not open our mouths and let Eva do the dazzling.

"Excuse me, Ma'am?" said Eva with her sweetest, feigned smile.

"Yes?" snapped the receptionist. The knowledge of three children in front of her desk did not soften her heart.

"Hello! Before I go further, I must compliment your dressing sense," said Eva, this time with feigned surprise. "That *dupatta* definitely highlights your skin tone, and goes beautifully with the *kurta* too!" By this time, Eric and I had joined in the drama too.

"Really? I was quite sceptical of wearing this one in the morning," returned the receptionist, calmer now.

"I can assure you, Ma'am, you have no reason to be sceptical," Eva said this with a conviction so solid that it would have made an ogre feel beautiful. "Moreover, with a charming face like yours, any piece of linen would look magnificent on you." Done. The foundation had been laid.

"Aren't you a flatterer," blushed the receptionist, laughing and disclosing her cavity-stricken teeth. '*At least she is loved by germs and insects,*' I thought.

"Certainly not, Ma'am. I'm just telling you the truth." It became harder by each minute to stifle our giggles. "Now, if you could be so good as to help us out, please, Ma'am?" said Eva with a perfectly guileless expression a pair of eyes could possibly bear.

"Yes, of course, darling!" the receptionist replied in a voice not inured to the futile and contemptible practice of kindness.

"Our friend was admitted here earlier today. We would like to know which room he is in."

"I'll look him up. What's his name?" This must have been her first straight reply in her entire life.

"Vihaan."

"He was admitted today morning at 8 o'clock, for a concussion, in all likelihood. He's in room number 21 on the second floor. The first room on your left."

"Okay, thank you so much!" Eva exclaimed with exultation at discovering the routes to a secret treasure.

As we left the receptionist behind, we exchanged glances that could not but betray our delight at Eva's propensity of being the "good girl" and an occasional sycophant. Our precariously stifled giggles had transformed our faces to freshly plucked tomatoes, which would have conveniently exposed our game had the receptionist resolved upon her life to play against our luck and looked up from her desk. But thankfully, she didn't and complied with our luck. We crossed the reception area and met the stairs. The ground floor had the lobby and twenty normal wards, while the floor above had five operation theatres, two ICUs and another fifteen normal wards. Going by the statistics and financial prospects of hospitals owned by the neighbouring villages, our hospital could be considered affluently sophisticated if the statistics of these other hospitals were drowning and the financial prospects already drenched in futility.

We reached our desired floor and followed the instructions given by the receptionist of the room's exact location.

"What if Vihaan's parents are inside?" I whispered, nervously.

"What if they don't approve of me and Eric?" asked Eva, equally nervous.

"What if they humiliate us and throw us out?" asked Eric, seemingly more anxious.

"Well, they won't humiliate Tamanna; and definitely won't throw her out. Their son is going to marry her sister," observed Eva.

"So that makes us even more vulnerable, doesn't it?" said Eric. Our nerves climbed another level when the door was suddenly flung open by Rihan Bhaiya.

"Hello!" He greeted us softly but congenially, peeked behind his back to assure himself of no potential danger, and gently closed the door behind him so as to not claim any unsolicited attention.

"You've come here to meet Vihaan, I assume?" he asked with an affable smile. His demeanour calmed our pulse to a normal rate, and we heaved a sigh of relief.

"Thank God it's just you, and not one of the monsters," blurted Eric.

"Eric!" Eva and I exclaimed in a loud whisper, aghast by his impulsivity and impropriety.

"What?" Eric asked looking at us, still bewildered about what accounted for this outburst. His eyes then shifted to Rihan Bhaiya and realisation finally dawned on his ambiguous mind. "Oh! I'm sorry! I didn't realise..." And he trailed off.

"What didn't you realise? That he is a tangible specimen of the human species with proper functioning ears which can perfectly relay any message to his brain because of his thoroughly operational auditory receptors, and that this specimen is standing not even half a metre away from us right now and is therefore, has been experiencing the aforementioned process all this while, and might also be the brother-in-law of the girl whom you so effortlessly and impeccably embarrassed a second ago by completely surpassing the frame of being insufferably impetuous? Which part of it did you not realise, Eric?" I lashed out at him.

"I...," Eric started when Eva intervened.

"Shut up if you value your life," Eva warned, and Eric placed a finger on his lips.

"Hey!" Rihan Bhaiya brought our attention to his tangible form now. "It's alright. Eric merely called them what I have always believed but could never dare to bring it to my lips. He has actually taken a burden off this human specimen," Rihan Bhaiya smiled at me and gave Eric a playful wink, who immediately brightened up at this but one glare from me restored him and his finger back to their former state. He continued in a much softer tone and warm eyes, "He didn't embarrass you in the least, Tamanna. All of you can talk to me as freely as you want, and you don't have to be afraid of your sister's and my engagement breaking off and you or your friends being held responsible for it. No one will ever blame you if we were ever to be disengaged. I assure you this." I was astonished when my unspoken fears were so eloquently vanquished by Rihan Bhaiya. It wasn't his words, but rather his manner, which could have brought a weeping child to ease, let alone an insecure and apprehensive seven-year-old. '*So, this is how a brother is supposed to be like…*'

"Shall we go inside now?" asked Rihan Bhaiya.

"No! First, tell us what brought him to the hospital. What happened today morning?" urged Eva.

"Oh, just another unusually natural day! Vihaan and I got into an argument with our parents about my marriage which escalated into this (he said, jerking his head towards the closed room) when our father pushed Vihaan away – he was standing in front of me like a bodyguard," he chuckled lightly, "as he moved toward me with clenched fists. The push sent your lean, malnutrition-struck friend headlong into the wall."

"Won't your parents object to Eric and me? And weren't you going somewhere when you came out of the room?" Eva inquired after another one of our relatable-reality-hit pauses.

"I'll deal with my parents if they object; and yes, I was supposed to buy certain medicines for Vihaan, but they aren't very urgent. Come in now."

He opened the door to a forlorn Vihaan, a praying mother counting her beads and a preoccupied father traversing the length of the room – it was the lull before another storm. Vihaan was awake; his eyes had found something engaging on the ceiling to prevent him from noticing the creaking of the door. His mother had dived too deep into her prayers to give any trifling activity outside her mind the power to pull her back to the surface. This left only the father awake and conscious enough to respond to the meek creak of the door.

"Good that you brought the medicines, Rihan. You stay here. I'll go and talk to the doctor," he said, still savouring the floor.

"We have some guests," Rihan Bhaiya replied curtly. At this, he looked up at us and his expression changed from sudden and absolute attention to a repulsive realisation and ultimately, loathing, when his eyes arrived on Eva and Eric. Vihaan detached himself from the ceiling too and the melancholy on his face was instantly replaced by an unparalleled joy. The pious woman's attention still couldn't be secured.

"What are these two doing here?" asked the father; his eyes sprinting between Eva and Eric. Fortunately or unfortunately, this question was enough to rouse the devotee from her religious reverie.

"We...we...we have come to meet Vihaan," I said, stammering.

"It's fine for you to come, considering he's the brother of your future brother-in-law," said the mother, looking at me, "but I don't see what these other two (she fumbled here, seemingly at a loss of words to refer to Eva and Eric) – whatever they are – are doing here."

"Friends. They are my friends," prompted Vihaan with a conviction unlikely for a person who had suffered a concussion a few hours prior. "And I'm not only the brother to Tamanna's future brother-in-law. I'm her *friend* as well. Are you not aware of this word?" he questioned his mother mockingly.

"Vihaan!" bellowed his father. "Is this how you talk to the woman who has been endlessly praying for you since you banged your head in the morning?"

"It might do the "woman" well if she prayed for some sense, rather than me. I have several others who wish well for me and care about me."

"Shut up!" His father's voice rose to another decibel. "That's your mother you're talking about!"

"I know. That is exactly what I regret." Vihaan's composure was frightening me; because I knew a single crack in this composure would unleash a myriad of emotions that had been stifled in the pits of his heart. This was one thing all of us had been blessed with in equal proportion – dysfunctional families and oblivious parents.

"Are you insulting your mother for these two schmucks?" asked his mother in a scarily menacing whisper.

"It's impossible for you to have any respect for anyone, isn't it?" said Rihan Bhaiya, disappointed.

"I have more love and respect for my *friends* than I have for you, and this ratio is broadening with each passing second," said Vihaan, glaring at his mother, with utter resentment and contempt kindling in his eyes.

"Shut up! Rihan, you are his elder brother. You are supposed to talk sense into him and not assist him in his imbecility," retorted the mother.

"You are assisting your husband in his imbecility, if not leading him. I'm only in support and full agreement of what my brother is saying because he's finally speaking, not only his, but both our minds – something which the compliant coward in me never allowed me to do," replied Rihan Bhaiya with a straight, unwavering face.

"All this education and running around with these schmucks has completely corroded your brains!" yelled the wise mother.

"Stop calling them "schmucks." They are my friends and you have no right to demean them." The composure was now on the verge of cracking.

"Enough!" Once again bellowed the bull. "Do you not understand, Vihaan? These termites are filling your head with all sorts of rubbish against your own family."

"NO!" cracked the composure. "*YOU TWO* (his eyes moving between his parents) are the termites who are slowly and viciously eating away my life and my brother's life! You are like weeds – you suffocate us! You make me regret ever having a family! You've already destroyed Bhaiya's life by not allowing him to go to the city and make a life of his own there. You've cemented a leash around his neck and tied him to this rotten place in a rotten house with a rotten family! And my life? I am only seven years old, and I have as many regrets as a seventy-year-old man who could achieve nothing in his life and is now on his deathbed. You've made my life a paradox – I have parents, yet I feel like an orphan because I'd rather have no parents than two people in disguise of it whose only mission in life is to wreck mine! I am simply a burden on you which will be attenuated only after I start earning and leave your *hellish house!*"

"Shut UP, Vihaan!" And the benevolent father proceeded to slap his already-suffering-from-a-concussion son. The slap reverberated through the walls of the room – screaming anguish and affliction and imploring deliverance from a merciless, oblivious and torturous family. What shook me to the core was Vihaan's reaction to the slap – a smile. That was not an ordinary, happy smile. That was the smile adorned by someone who was satisfied; satisfied with proving his point to himself and to the world; satisfied with a decision he could see materialise in the future; satisfied with the unsaid contract being finally signed.

"Are you insane?" yelled Rihan Bhaiya and shoved his father to the wall; a trifle more hostility and the word "threw" would have been more appropriate. "Can you not see what state he's in? How DARE you slap him?"

"If he's in a good enough state to declare himself an orphan, then he's in a good enough state to receive a slap too! And don't ask me how I dared to slap my own son! I have all rights over him to do whatever I like!"

"NO, YOU DON'T! Do you not understand? Why doesn't something as simple as this get inside your small brain that you ARE NOT WORTH being called a FATHER?" Rihan Bhaiya was red with this overwhelming confrontation. He paused to regain his breath and recollect his thoughts and continued in a much calmer and surer voice, "Today, you didn't lose just one son, but both your sons. And it's you, and solely you who is to be blamed for this," he concluded with gritted teeth.

"This is all because of you!" spoke the devoted mother – glaring at Eva and Eric. Well, she had to, since she hadn't contributed anything for a while. "This wouldn't have happened if you hadn't come here! Get out of the room NOW!"

"They won't go anywhere! They are my friends and they've come to meet me!" said Vihaan.

"Be quiet, Vihaan! They will leave this room right now! Tamanna can stay back, but the other two won't. And Tamanna," she turned towards me, "I am definitely going to have a chat with your father regarding your company these days." The devoted mother was now devoted to me as well.

"Stop intruding in people's lives! Keep your nose to yourself, please!" retorted Vihaan.

"Her sister is going to marry your brother! I have every right to intrude in her life," the mother defended herself.

"Please be so kind as to explain to me – which imaginary rights do you and your husband keep talking of?" enquired Rihan Bhaiya.

"The *natural* rights which we gained when we gave birth to you, nurtured you, provided a roof over your head. What more do you need?" replied the mother.

"Okay. I'll free you of that right today itself. I'll buy a house in the city, and as soon as I find one, I'll move there. Also, I'll take Vihaan along with me. Till then, we are your guests, and nothing more," stated Rihan Bhaiya.

"I won't talk about this in front of strangers." This was the only reply the poor mother was capable of at that moment.

"But you can slap your own 'son' in front of 'strangers.' Sure!" mocked Vihaan. There was nothing left to say anymore. The brothers had given their verdict and shut their parents. But there was still one task left to accomplish.

"Get out of the room," and the loving woman threw Eva and Eric out of the room. Yes, the word has been rightly used here. She slammed the door behind her and glared at her lost sons.

"Seven-year-olds. *Merely* seven-year-olds; and that is how you treat them." Rihan Bhaiya was on the verge of tears. I hadn't seen a son so ashamed of his own mother.

"Those are my friends you *threw* out of the room," Vihaan said with as much menace in his voice as contempt in his eyes.

"No! They are just trash! And you are going to stay away from them if you value your life," his father threatened.

"Believe me, I live by an inexplicable and inexorable impulse of an independent execution of my actions. While I agree that it is very unfortunate that these impulses never overlap with YOUR desires, I wish to remain content with my impulses because they are definitely more cautiously and informatively guided than even your thinking brains. So, I beseech you with all my energy left after receiving your precious, invaluable gifts – the concussion, the arguments and the slap – to not fret over who I befriend and whose company I indulge in. It won't avail anything. You should rather exhibit your despotic and shallow practices where they are wholeheartedly accepted – if not venerated in the least – than bestow upon your ungrateful, prodigal son the privilege to consume all your golden, well-intentioned pieces of advice and statutes," Vihaan replied. His rejoinder – which received mixed responses from his audience – had transfixed us to our spots. On one end of the pole, were Rihan Bhaiya and I, beaming with pride at his explicit stance, while on the other hand, were his parents, who gave the impression of being robbed of their most invaluable and exquisite fortune, except they had never esteemed its worth, and therefore, bore a superficial qualm of being betrayed and deceived.

"Now, if you would please leave the room, I would love to have some peace with my brother and my friend," he requested, smiling.

"Why should we go?" asked the defeated mother in her relentless pursuit of boring her son.

"Because a sick patient is asking you to and I'll call the nurse to escort you out if you don't leave willingly in the next five seconds," Vihaan replied crisply. He had completely annihilated his parents. His delight over this triumph was as explicitly laid out on his face as the despots' defeat was weighing them down.

When they had left the room, I said, "Wow! Did you just lay your entire dictionary bare in front of them?"

"No; not my "entire" dictionary," he replied with a lopsided smile.

"That was really impressive," added Rihan Bhaiya.

"Well, it's a new trick I learnt today. They are as bereft of words as they are of logic, and while they are completely unaware of the latter fact, they are absolutely and wholeheartedly in possession of the former. So, if I can't beat them in their version of logic, I can anytime resort to words!" And after a long trial, the three of us shared a light moment in the midst of pure and untainted love.

I left the hospital after about fifteen minutes and found Eva and Eric mindlessly playing around with sticks and stones a few paces outside the hospital. "How's Vihaan? When will they discharge him?" enquired Eva as I approached them.

"He's alright. He lectured his parents – not an outburst, but very formally – just after his mother pushed you out and he ordered his parents to leave the room as well. The remaining three of us talked for a while. Dr Adam entered after a few minutes and advised me to go home and let him rest. Rihan Bhaiya will be staying with him tonight. He'll be discharged tomorrow probably. The concussion wasn't very serious. His parents will be leaving soon too, so we better get away from here."

"Yes, let's go to Dadu's. We have to give them the news too," advised Eric.

We gave the hospital building one last look to conclude the day and were on our way, when Eric asked me, "Are you still angry?"

"About? With? Why?" I asked.

"About the monster statement; with me; because that was rude and impulsive," Eric replied with a sullen face.

"Yes."

"I'M SORRY! I truly am! I hadn't thought it out and just blurted out what came to my mouth!" he groaned.

"Impulsivity is never 'thought out', Eric. That is the reason it is called 'impulsive'. And your thoughtlessness and impulsivity would have put me in terrible danger today had it not been for Rihan Bhaiya's good nature."

"Yes, I know that! And that is exactly why I am so terribly sorry! I'll be more careful next time, I promise!"

"Okay! Stop whining like a baby!"

"So, you forgive me? You are not angry anymore?" he asked, excited.

"No," I replied with a playful side grin.

"YAY!" And he jumped on top of me and suddenly we were rolling on the ground, roaring our hearts out, shrouded in dust. Somewhere, in the back of our minds, we knew what awaited us once we got home – the interrogations for the dirty dress and scrapes in the hands and legs, the "Is this how a girl should behave?" and "Who were you with?" sermons, and then the useless bickering and punishment – but at that moment, the looming repercussions were the least of our concerns, because, at the end of the day, these repercussions were for the sake of the people who taught me the meaning of love and kept my heart alive.

We brushed ourselves clean after Eva pulled us up, holding our sleeves and reprimanding us for "behaving like children," being the mother of our group. We resumed our journey when Eric turned towards me and said, "Tamanna, the next time you feel compelled to deliver a harangue, please keep it simple and to be easily understood by us – the common people – whose source of words are not books but their friends."

"Where did you learn "harangue" from?" I asked, laughing.

"Ashwat Sir had once given me a pile of books to return to the library. There was a dictionary in it too. So, while I was stacking the books on the shelf, the dictionary fell, and it opened the first page for 'h.' I bent down to pick it up and just glanced over the page. I remember the word from there."

"Wow. If only you had as much sensibility as you have brains," Eva chimed in, giggling.

That night, in the hospital, the two brothers had a discussion, about which I came to know much later.

"Why can't they simply break it off if you and Durga Didi don't want this?" was Vihaan's question.

"They can't because we have reached the "appropriate marriage age." If Durga doesn't get married now, she might not find a respectable man later and their family can no longer afford to support four children. So, they're marrying off their older burden. As for me, she's simply a very compatible match, according to our priest, of course – one I might not receive ever again."

"And the interests of the two people whose lives are going to be most affected by this should not be taken into account?"

"No."

"Why?"

"Because we're still children and don't know what's good for us."

"What a load of crap!"

"What else do you think all of this is? There probably isn't a single house in these villages which isn't wrought with violence and degradation; not a single house where its girls and women are not considered a burden; not a single house which doesn't harbour prejudices – whether implicit or explicit – against the other sex or religion or caste or class; not a single house which values and comprehends the significance or the gravity of proper education; not a single house which can appreciate the institution of a family; and not a single house which can fathom the fact that every individual is capable of *thinking for themselves!*"

Vihaan took a long pause to digest everything that constituted "crap," and asked, "Can't we do anything about this?"

"We can't change the mindset of the elders – their brains are beyond repair. What we *can* do is prevent our generation from treading along the path of the previous generations, encourage them to have a mind of their own, identify the evils within their families and villages and pledge to redress them. And don't think that it hasn't started. Dr Adam, Ashwat Sir and Mahira Ma'am are illustrative of new and better times – of a more uplifting and supportive society."

"I wish I could do something too."

"You will in the years to come," Rihan Bhaiya consoled, giving his warmest smile. "You should sleep now. It was a hectic day. Get some rest."

"Every day is a hectic day. What's new about it?" Vihaan sighed. He closed his eyes and gradually surrendered himself to his dreams.

11

FROM EVA'S EYES

"Eva! Get some water from the well, will you?" asked Mum from the kitchen.

"I'm studying right now, Mum! I'll go after a while," I replied. In the silence that ensued for the next five minutes, the only sound which breached it was the cluttering of the utensils Mum was placing in the racks after washing them. The next sound halted the silence for a while, but not for too long.

"Eva, when are you planning to get the water?" Mum asked again.

"After I finish this topic," I replied, engrossed in my book, completely oblivious that Mum was unaware of "this."

The tainted silence returned, only to be shattered after another five minutes.

"Eva!" This time, Mum yelled.

"What?" I jerked my head up, as though somebody had snatched me away from a different world and brought me back to my house.

"This is the third time I'm asking you to fetch some water from the well!"

"And this is the third time I'm telling you that I'll go once I finish what I'm studying," I retorted.

"We have to cook lunch, Eva! Is that book of yours more important than lunch?" Mum asked. Her belittling tone provided the implication much more than her words ever could.

"Yes Mum, this *book of mine* is more important to me than *cooking* because I love studying and reading! Cooking is a burden to me! And why don't you send Eric if it's so important? He isn't doing anything productive."

"He's napping. Why should I wake someone up when there's someone else who is awake and is equally capable of completing the job?"

"*Napping?* Who on Earth naps at 10:30 in the morning? And you are not ready to wake your prince up from his sleep, but you are ready to disturb my studies?"

"Studies can be done later," Mum said sternly through gritted teeth.

"As if 'naps' cannot be taken later."

Just then the prince, my brother, came out of the room, rubbing his eyes, and asked in a whiny voice, "Why are you screaming so much early in the morning?"

"Because you were sleeping and just so you know, it is well past 'early morning.' So, wake up now," I replied, glaring at him.

"Shut up, Eva. Eric, your sister won't go to the well. Hence, the shouting."

"Why?" Eric asked through crescent eyes.

"Because I was studying!" I stressed once again. Turning back to my mother, I elaborated, "And I never said that I *won't* go to the well. I said I *will*, but *after* I'm done studying a particular topic."

"Mum, you could have simply woken me up instead of pestering her. You know she doesn't like getting interrupted when she's studying." The most genuine intentions can sometimes come off as deliberate derision.

"Oh sure! She is the queen of the country and the queen should never be disturbed! What else am I supposed to do? Massage her hands and legs, complete her errands and become her slave? Tell me. What else?"

"No, Mum! I didn't mean it like that. Just like you don't like being disturbed while you're cooking, she doesn't like being disturbed while she's studying. It's as simple," Eric replied calmly with a shrug.

"How can you even think of comparing cooking with those books? Those books will take you nowhere; especially you (she had fixed her gaze on me)! You NEED to learn how to cook if you want a husband and a good life! I could make entire meals when I was your age!"

"It's strange that you associate a 'good life' with having a husband, while *your* husband has given you nothing but debts, bruises, unhappiness and anxiety as constant companions," I retorted.

Mum advanced towards me brusquely, with her right-hand muscles taut and fury encompassing the lengths of her face. She raised her hand in the air, which, had it fallen on my face, would have left not only a beautiful imprint of my beautiful mother's beautiful hand on my petty face but would have also left me hugging the floor. Luckily, God decided to grace me at that very instant and sent our father barging in through the door.

"What is going on?" he asked, shocked and breathless (as if he hadn't ever seen or participated in the act of beating one's own children). "Well, whatever it is, I don't care." He paused for a second, looking around the house as though searching for something other than intelligible words and sentences. "Oh, and also, stop it right away." He found the right words but couldn't muster the right intention.

"Are you looking for something?" Mum asked Papa.

"Do you have any money hidden anywhere?" Papa asked nervously, evading Mum's questioning eyes.

"Why will I hide any money? Whatever wage you get, I keep it safely in the box, even without counting," Mum replied carelessly.

"Okay, okay. No need to blabber," Papa said, picking up jars and random boxes, foraging the dust and dirt under each potential hiding place.

"I'm not *blabbering*! I'm simply telling you that I *do not hide* any money! So…" Mum's explanation was interrupted by a curt knock on the door. Papa jumped so hard at this and swerved to face the door that he dropped the tiny Russian doll, underneath which, he seemed sure to find gold had he been allowed to peruse the shelf a little while longer.

"Is your husband here? We need to talk to him," asked a man as Mum pulled open the door. The man sounded polite but stern, speaking with a sense of finality. He was tall and well-built with visibly peeking biceps and triceps, as though they were his surrogate eyes, viewing and interacting with the world through his arms. The walls of our house could be easily shattered by the mercy of this man's hands. He was accompanied by two other men – each as burly and brawny than the other, but not as much as the first man. There was one more similarity that all three of them shared – the dumb, unspeaking, expressionless eyes. The surrogate eyes would have probably soon taken over their masters.

"He's inside. Why?" replied Mum, dubious and eager to know what was happening and what was going to happen in her house.

"Here, here! I'm here!" called out Papa and went to greet the men with a nervous smile. "Aren't you going to ask them inside, dear?" Papa asked Mum with a feigned smile, his eyes trying to convey what his words were avoiding.

"I will once they tell me who they are and what business they have here," Mum replied defiantly.

"Didn't you tell your wife who we are and what business we have here, Robin?" asked the first man innocently looking at Papa. "No worries. Now that I'm here, I'll tell her on my own." He fixed Mum with his sudden attention. Even though I felt a touch of imbecility in his attitude while he was talking to Papa, his demeanour betrayed nothing but absolute resignation to Mum's authority beyond the threshold of the house when he turned to face her. He sounded confident, with an undertone of palpable regard, when he spoke to her, "Ma'am, your husband is obliged to work in my field a minimum of three hours a day, earning five rupees for the first three hours, and two rupees for each consequent hour."

"But why? He has his own field to work on!" Mum asked.

"I know. I was coming to that. As you probably know, your harvest in this last season wasn't adequate to be sold in the market with a profit. So, he borrowed money from me – a hundred rupees – with an interest of twenty per cent, which he was supposed to pay within four months."

"Is twenty per cent a lot?" she whispered in Papa's ears.

"As compared to other moneylenders, no, it isn't." The man had impeccable hearing too. "So, to pay off his debt to me, he took an extra job and began working in my field – sometimes five to six hours a day. You'll be glad to know that your husband was very persistent and dedicated and might have also cleared his debt by the end of the four months, but he lost some of the money he had earned at the market in gambling. He was supposed to pay the fees of his children's school with that money. This led to the burden of another loan because his children would have been kicked out of school if he hadn't paid the fees. So, he took the loan from me at a smaller interest this time, since it was a matter of his children's education – fifteen per cent – and promised to repay me within five months. It had been three months of the first loan when he took the second loan. Today marks the fifth month of the first loan. A week hence, it'll be the second month of the second loan. Your husband was very irregular to work two months back and has been completely absent from work since this past month. So, naturally, I assume your husband has found a higher-paying job somewhere else, and is now ready with my money." He turned to face Papa after speaking this last line. "Can we come in, now, Ma'am?" he asked Mum with a smile that left her with no other answer but a faint, "Yes."

The three men came inside and suddenly our house felt too small and fragile to bear the weight of three bulky men. The air felt suffocating; the feeble rustling of the leaves felt noisy; the chirping of the birds seemed like an unwarranted ruckus and the general hustle and bustle of the world outside sounded like a disturbing commotion. Despite the light breeze flowing from the window, I found myself profusely sweating.

"I think the children should go inside their room. They shouldn't be present when the elders talk," stated the man after a fleeting glance at us.

"Yes, I completely agree with you, Sir!" acknowledged Papa like a mindless disciple. "Go inside the two of you! Eva, take these books along with you. Don't make the house a mess when there are guests present."

"Okay, Papa," Eric and I chorused.

We went inside our room, closed the door, laid the books on the bed and stuck our ears on the door. The man spoke with an uncanny calmness that made us strain our ears to the extent that they would have dissolved with the wood if science had allowed them to do so.

"So, Robin, do you have the money?" the man asked without beating around the bush.

"What's the hurry? I'll give you your money, Sir!" Papa replied with a conviction that even the tiniest morsel of his heart could not feel. "Why don't you eat something first? My wife will arrange some snacks for you!"

A momentary silence pursued – a silence heavy with an impatient dread. The only spores of lucidity in this silence were the occasional clattering of dishes, hitting against each other.

"No need," the man's voice lifted the heaviness. "I had a heavy breakfast. I'm not hungry right now. I came here with a purpose, and I don't like it when my purposes are not fulfilled." The man stopped, waiting for a response.

"I would really insist you eat at least *something*, Sir! My wife is a wonderful cook! You'll regret your entire life that you refused food cooked by *her!*"

"What is Papa doing?" I asked Eric anxiously. "Why is he evading this man? Just give him the money and let him out of the house!" My voice was choking. I didn't know exactly why. I was never very close to my parents, nor did I ever feel any familial love towards them. Also, I had dealt with men of his like in the past. So, I shouldn't have been scared of him. Yet, I was.

"No, Robin. Did I not tell you that I'm full right now?" He was still speaking in the same monotone.

"Yes, Sir, but did I not tell you too that you'd regret not eating my wife's food?" Papa replied jokingly, in an attempt to lighten the atmosphere.

"You've always been such a sweet, humble man, Robin, always trying to please others. That's one reason why I'm so fond of you. But the bottom line is I am very particular about my transactions. Now, with people whom I dislike, I don't hesitate to extract my money using whatever means that pervade my imagination at that moment. But in the case of people I *do* like, I usually do not let my imagination take over me. So, my imagination is in your hands. Tell me, what should I do with it?" The man spoke with an eerie assurance – the assurance you get of the gigantic waves at the heart of the ocean while standing at its coast.

"Well, Sir, since you said it yourself that you're fond of me, I was hoping if you could give me some more time to pay you back. I'd be eternally grateful to you."

"Haven't I already given you two months extra?"

"Yes, Sir." Papa could feel his excuses diminishing, and his time ebbing away.

"Then?" He was still polite.

"I was…busy somewhere else. That is the reason why I was so irregular."

"May I know where?"

Papa scrupled. "I had found another gambling group. I earned a lot of money initially but lost all of it after two weeks. I was afraid to approach you after that."

"Well, Robin, don't you think you should have been more prudent with your decisions, considering you have a wife and two small children to support?"

"I committed a mistake, Sir."

"Yes, you did, and mistakes are supposed to be punished. Can I have a word with you outside?"

"Sure, Sir." We heard the creak of the door open and close behind them. The rusty noise of the latch followed. I couldn't restrain myself any longer and burst into the living room.

"Hey! What do you think you're doing – locking us in like this?" Mum unbridled her frustration of the entire morning on the door. She would have definitely broken it down had she not been so little and frail.

"They locked us in?" Eric cried. "Why would they do something like that?"

"Stop bashing the door, Mum! Try listening to their conversation." Taking in a deep, anxious breath, she complied.

"I can't hear anything."

"Eric, go to the door and see if you can hear anything. I'll watch out the window," I said.

The window was in the wall adjacent to the one which held the door. I couldn't get a clear view even if the men stood at some distance from the door. We remained motionless for a couple of minutes. In those couple of minutes, I could hear the wind chasing the birds, the ants scuttering away with their food, the dust being picked off the ground and unified with the wind, Mum's nervous breathing from where she stood and most distinctly, the thudding of my heart. I didn't know what I expected to see outside the window, nor did Mum and Eric know what they expected to hear, but there was a collective instinct that resisted compliance with our forced sense of reassurance. We stood straining our senses and necks till I saw a faint streak of blood, slowly impregnating my eyes. A wave of dread drenched me. '*What if that's…*'

"Break the door," I said in a terse whisper.

"What?" asked Eric.

"Break the door."

"Have you lost your mind? I am a small, weak woman and you are a couple of seven-year-olds. How are we supposed to break the door?" Mum snapped.

"I don't know!" I panicked. "What I *do* know is that I can see blood and I'm pretty damn sure that's Papa's!" Mum rushed over to the window and shoved me aside. I could see her face changing colour from alarm and incredulity to a harrowing realisation. Unlike the frailer minds of the world, she picked up the saddle quern and braced herself for a full-fledged attack at the door without wasting a second more. She groaned through clenched teeth as she picked it up and I could see her veins trying to break free from her skin and her blood gushing to her face, turning it a deep red.

"Move aside, Eric!" Mum screamed.

She hurled herself at the door with all the might her God could suffuse in her at that moment. The next thing we heard was the crashing of the door against her resolute mind and bare physique. She had reduced half the door into rubble in just a matter of seconds.

"Eva! Take this." She handed me the quern. "Eric, help me get your father inside."

The entire village had gathered there to derive drama out of our predicament, but not a single soul offered to help Mum. They stood there, a foot away from the door, gaping at the unprecedented theatrics of the morning. I could hear hushed whispers being delivered from one ear to another. There was a nonchalant amusement in their eyes, arising out of a heedless conviction for the arrival of this day, an unconscious eagerness for a diversion from their otherwise monotonous lives. It's strange – the difference between *knowing* the superficiality of the world, and *experiencing* it. You *know* it exists, but you'll know how buoyantly it thrives once it starts thriving on you like a virus. I wanted to scream at them, but I didn't. I wanted to tell them how despicable their lot were, but I didn't. I wanted to show them how repulsed I was by the sight of them, but I didn't. All of this would have given an impression of vulnerability. I didn't want that. I didn't want to bare myself naked in front of these stone-carved effigies. Rather, I chose to be indifferent. Screaming and yelling would have meant that they mattered, but it's the feeling of being utterly trivial and inconsequential that exasperates the most. That is exactly what I wanted them to feel.

"Shall we get you some mattresses and snacks too? You can enjoy the play to your heart's content then," Eric snapped at them.

"Eric! Come inside! Mum, let's take Papa inside our room."

It was only when we had laid him down on our mattress that I could bring myself to fix my glance on him. To be precise, Papa was relatively unhurt from what all those three men seemed – and probably would have been, if not for some mysterious restraining element – capable of. Papa's bruises seemed too accurately calculated. He had a dominant left side, and while there was not a single assault mark on his left leg, they weren't exactly as merciful to his left hand. Similarly, while there were several swellings and purple spots on his bloody face, they had carefully circumvented his forehead, and upon examination, his head too.

"Eva, you could at least help me instead of staring at your father like that!" Mum said, panting through the room as she brought a vessel filled with water up to the brim and a bottle of antiseptic liquid.

"Yes, Mum!" I replied robotically.

"Go and bring some bandages, cotton and ointment. Eric, help your sister. Make sure she doesn't immerse herself in another one of her books or stand gazing at the broken door."

"Mum! You don't…" I began.

"Shush! Keep quiet and let's just do as she says," Eric whispered to me sternly, tightly clasping my arm, and pulled me out of the room.

An hour later, Papa was finally worth looking at. We had cleaned up his wounds, given him some juice and propped him up on our pillow. None of the wounds seemed particularly life-threatening so the hospital was out of question. "Hospital? What more will it do except extract money from us?" was Mum's reply upon being asked if Papa should be taken to the hospital.

After a while, Papa spoke, "You're an intelligent girl, aren't you, Eva? Well, at least your teacher says so. How would I know? I'm a simple man whose only contribution was bringing you to this world. I wouldn't know if you were the next Satyajit Ray or C.V. Raman, would I? I barely attended school and have only heard about these names, let alone read. But you can read, can't you? Hell, you can write too! Your teacher once told me that you write very well! That means you can write your own sentences too! You read books I could never even dream of touching, let alone *peruse*. Did I use that right? I guess I did. You talk about subjects I have never even heard of, let alone think about. You use words I can't pronounce even after fifty rounds of practice. 'Peroos' is an exception probably. Although I still don't know if I'm using or pronOUncing it right. Hey! I finally said THAT right! PronOUncing! Wow! I'm getting better!"

"Papa, what are you saying? Don't you think you should just rest right now? We'll talk tomorrow morning," I said, worried for his eloquent, but not exactly pointless, balderdash. I was worried about what he was arriving at and what implications his conclusion would bring upon me.

"Oh, no, no! I'm perfectly alright to talk. I might not be alright to gamble – as he said – but I can still learn to use my right hand. I might not be able to walk properly for a few days – as he said – but my left leg is pretty strong. It'll bear it. Also, I have been spared my brain, so I can still use it and think – as he said."

"As *who* said?" Mum asked, exasperated.

"Why? Did you not hear? I heard perfectly well! In fact, I guess I can still hear him," Papa replied, absent-mindedly.

"Hear WHOM?" the three of us asked in a chorus. Papa rapidly blinked his eyes, as though our chagrin had awakened him from his stupor.

"Brian! The moneylender! He came to our house today with his two men to ask for his money. Did you not see him? Of course, you saw him! He told you two to go to your rooms (Papa said looking at me and Eric) and answered your incessant queries and also refused your snacks (Papa said looking at Mum). Have you forgotten him so soon?" Papa replied in a matter-of-factly way.

"No, we haven't forgotten him. But you're not talking sense! Why don't you rest for now and we'll talk later," Mum said.

"But I'm absolutely fine! I don't want to rest!" Papa protested.

"I don't think that I gave you a choice. Rest!" Mum commanded.

What we had not anticipated was the sudden vicissitude that followed. Papa's stupor was, after all, feigned. We had very conveniently overlooked the couched rage, humiliation and powerlessness that had kept stabbing the thick veil through the morning, harder with every passing second, till it finally tore, snatching the breath out of us with its effortlessly unfettered ferocity.

He slapped Mum with the back of his right hand, in which he habitually wore three thin, but sharp rings. I stared at him, aghast. At that moment, I was not frightened of him. I was repelled; disgusted – disgusted with the sudden awareness of being his daughter; disgusted with living in his house; disgusted with every atom which he had touched in his entire lifetime; disgusted with the air he breathed and the words he spoke. It would have been less painful if my eyes had bled when he slapped the woman who had not just surrendered her life to him but had also lost in him her mind, body and soul, than being privy to a barbarian's mercy. Mercy, because each action of his guaranteed something larger – so large that it made the former look small, paltry. It made him merciful because his ruthlessness was capable of supreme infinity.

"You wanted to know what I was saying, didn't you?" So, his balderdash was not pointless; nor were my worries.

"Yes."

"You little *brat!*" If only the men had not spared him his two other limbs. He limped towards me and hurled me across the room with the back of his perfectly functional right hand.

"If you're so intelligent, you have already probably noticed that they "punished" me only on my left hand and right leg. Want to know why? Because this is the hand I might have raised on the woman of my house. Want to know how he knew that? He had seen these rings in my right hand – the hand which I use less – and not on my left hand because I use it more. Moreover, he saw red marks on your mother's face – the "remnants" of the last time she dared to misbehave. Did I use that word right – "remnants"? Coming to my right leg – well my left leg is stronger, so I'll have my stronger leg even if something happens to my weaker leg and I lose it. I'll still be able to walk around and 'earn for my family' and '*edyucate*' my children. Did I pronounce that right? Is it '*edyucate*' or '*edoocate*' or '*educaite*?*' Whatever it is, I don't give a damn. I don't care. Well, to be '*precaaise*,' I don't care about the woman of my house and my daughter. So, even if I do work, it'll be purely for my SON! As soon as I'm able to walk on my two legs again – if ever that happens – I'll go to your school and get your name uh, uh, uh… What do you call it?"

I felt numb, as if I was receding into an abyss, a smothering unknown. The word "erudition" had been imprinted in my memory the first time I had heard it; knowing its meaning only made the imprint deeper and more fervent. It hasn't faded since. My school helped me dream of a life out of this village and of a world slightly closer to what I had read about a utopia. It made me feel that I'm not a solitary ant in a desert, but a star that can lighten up a dense night-sky. It gave me the most endearing moments of my life: with my friends, my teacher, my books, and the library. If I were to define my conception of "school" as something more compact, these would be the poles which gave meaning to my existence, around which my life revolved, and on which I had envisaged my rise.

"I. HATE. YOU." Papa didn't hear it as much as he felt it – the hate. My face probably revealed much more than my screaming voice ever could. I saw it in Papa's eyes – the shock, the ego crashing down noiselessly, the realisation of his daughter ebbing further away to the irrevocable and the realisation that he never was her father. I don't know what I saw more, the hurt or the final dawn. But Papa's eyes betrayed all of it. They welled up when he realised that I didn't feel the slightest bit of remorse or regret for what I had said, as though I had truly meant that sentence, every part of it. His eyes now seemed like two moist, watery balls of fire – a fire able to neither wreck nor heal. The fire stopped him from drowning himself in his own tears, and the water tried to hold back an incensed eruption.

I got up and ran out of the house. I couldn't stay in the same room as that man who was supposedly my father. Fleeing from his presence had never felt easier. I felt an immense lightness when I came out of the house – a sense of freedom. It was temporary but overwhelming. I wanted to cry and rejoice at the same time. I couldn't choose what I wanted to do more. This dilemma numbed me while I kept running towards the mango tree.

As I was running out of the house, I heard Eric say, "You're horrible." He caught up with me and asked, "Want to race?"

"Yes." I doubled my speed and ran, indifferent to anyone who crossed my racetrack. I had no idea who had surpassed whom. I had no idea how far away Eric and I were. But I didn't want to stop. I wanted to keep running – as far as I could from that house, that wretched man, my village; and as close to absolute freedom as my feet could take me. *'If only I could fly, I wouldn't have to stop.'*

But I couldn't fly, and I had to stop. I reached the mango tree and found Tamanna and Vihaan there. I stopped in front of them abruptly – my face a wetland of perspiration and tears.

"Hey! Why were you running? And why are you all red?" Tamanna asked.

"Come and sit here," Vihaan pulled me by the elbow and sat me down between him and Tamanna.

"How do you run so fast?" Eric was behind me. He was struggling for breath when Vihaan asked, "Why were the two of you running?"

"Sit, Eric," Tamanna said, thumping the ground. "Tell us what happened."

Eric narrated the trajectory of the entire day to Vihaan and Tamanna. They listened, without interrupting, wide-eyed. They weren't shocked. They were disgusted, appalled. The thought of having an abusive gambler as a father was not unimaginable to them, nor was it unfamiliar; only abhorrent.

The howling silence that ensued after Eric had finished his narration didn't strain any of us. Vihaan and Tamanna were not searching for words to respond. They simply wrapped me in their arms with a softness that killed the desire in me to hear any word of consolation. It wasn't pity that they felt. You feel pity for someone inferior to you, someone who doesn't possess or can't possess what you have. But I wasn't inferior to them, nor did they ever engage in self-pity. They simply waited for me to heal, to climb out of the chasm I'd been pushed into.

"We won't let it happen," Tamanna spoke after fifteen minutes. They removed their hands, and I sat up straight, wiping my face.

"What?" I asked, gasping.

"We won't let you compromise on your education."

"How?"

"We'll talk to Ashwat Sir. He'll find a way out. We'll bring you our notes. We'll borrow whatever books you want from the library. We'll do whatever it takes to not disengage you from your passion."

"Yes. We'll do whatever it takes," Vihaan assured.

"Let's go to Dadu's. We'll get you something to eat and drink," said Eric.

"Okay." And we spent the rest of the evening at Dadu's.

12

A SCHOOL, A HOSPITAL AND A MISSION

Incidentally, the next day was a Saturday. No school. It was one of those Saturdays when the school was closed but the library wasn't. While we were on a break, Ashwat Sir's mind wasn't. It was nine in the morning and the six of us went to the library in search of him. Our library, just like our hospital, was much better off when compared to the libraries of neighbouring schools. The most surprising aspect of our library was not the quality of the books. They're already given primacy due to Ashwat Sir's stubborn influence and recurring arguments with the Principal. It was our librarian, Mahira Ma'am. She was the most, and the only, educated female among the three villages. People mostly knew her by her name, her profession and her brown hair, which lit up whenever touched by the sun. Her surname and credentials seldom mattered.

Similar to Dr Adam and Ashwat Sir, she too, had completed her high school in the main city and pursued her higher studies from the United Kingdom. Before she could apply for a doctorate, she was called back to the village – with two degrees in her hand, and one unfulfilled degree gnawing at her heart – because her parents had fixed her marriage with a thirty-five-year-old man without informing her. She was the youngest of five siblings, and also the golden sheep in the charcoal-black family. When she returned to the village – at the age of twenty-four – both her parents had already been greeted by death twice. A third time would mean ultimate adieu to this world. They had to settle their youngest – and the most impossible – daughter before boarding the final flight.

The "prodigal" daughter – as referred to by the villagers – tried hard to not bring herself down by living up to her sobriquet. Her life had always been strenuous, and she had nothing to repent for. Now, she was faced with the biggest quandary of her life – should she agree to the marriage and forsake her passion, or deny the marriage and watch her decrepit parents die out of her overwhelming defiance? She devised and chose a rather morbid option – she agreed to the marriage on the condition that it wouldn't take place in the next six months.

"But Mahira, I don't know if your mother and I will survive till then." Her father had his concerns.

"I know." She knew they wouldn't.

And they didn't. Three months later, they cremated the father. Their mother became delusional after her husband's demise. She couldn't bear the separation and joined him in the afterworld the next month.

Thus was Mahira Ma'am's path cleared. She severed her ties with the next in line hurdles – her siblings – and also broke her engagement. She returned to the UK, earned a doctorate degree, and finally gave in to the entreaties of her roots. But where was an unmarried, twenty-eight-year-old woman supposed to live when her own family had ousted her from her house?

Having been brought up in an uncooperative and hostile family, she had learnt to keep her expectations low and individualism high. She built herself a small room in one of the corners of our library and earned a permit from the authorities to use the washroom facilities of the school whenever required. She became the prototype of an independent, modern, unethical and sordid woman. The village women abhorred and envied her, the village men wanted to beat and rape her to show her her place; the children adored her.

As we entered the library, we found her dusting the shelves and rearranging all the books.

"Mahira Ma'am?" said Eva.

"Hello!" Her grave face brightened up as she saw us. "What's my favourite gang doing here on a Saturday? Shouldn't you be playing right now?"

Yes, we were her favourite gang.

"We were looking for Ashwat Sir. Is he here?" asked Vihaan.

"Oh, yes. He's been here since eight o'clock. I'll be surprised if he doesn't marry a book one of these days. You'll find him at table 4."

"Okay, thank you!"

We found Ashwat Sir in Table 4, reading "The Large-Scale Structure of Space-Time" by Stephen Hawking. Ashwat Sir's history is not very different from Dr Adam's. His parents had an inter-caste marriage. While they were perfectly certain that they could endure any degree of denunciations as long as they were together, their conviction was probably not sturdy enough. The villagers' criticisms, which they were hitherto indifferent to, soon turned into insidious flagellations, slowly but persistently tarnishing and ruining their family. By the time Ashwat Sir was twelve, he had already decided to flee the second he was granted the chance to do so. By the age of fifteen, he could bear it no more and decided to move to the city. He has been living alone ever since. His parents took their lives when he was completing his graduation from the University of Oxford, UK. He often wondered if his parents would have done so had he not left them to pursue his studies. But this thought was never accompanied by regret. "At least they'll now be able to lead a life which they couldn't when they were alive. There won't be any villains in their story now," he would tell us. When he was still a child, he had wanted to run away – run away to a place where the air which had polluted his parents' happy marriage would not, and could not, touch him. But he came back – with a doctorate to his credit – not to avenge the villains, but to try and prevent them from turning villainous in somebody else's story.

As long as he lived, the villagers never failed to hide their keenness in his romantic life, if there ever was any. He was known among the masses as the "run-away, unmarried boy of the parents who killed themselves." Who has ever cared for qualifications and achievements?

"Hello, Sir!" we greeted.

"Hello!" He jerked as though we had awakened him from a trance. "Isn't it Saturday today? What are you doing here? Oh, no! Did I misread the calendar again?"

"Yes, Sir, you did. We've been waiting for you since morning," Eric replied with a straight face.

"Isn't it a bit irresponsible on your part, Sir?" I asked, gravely.

"Oh no, no, no, no!" He got up and started collecting his stuff carelessly. "The Principal will not spare me this time!" he said with furrowed brows.

"What if he expels you, Sir?" Vihaan asked.

"Yes, Sir. Where will you go then? Whom will you teach?" asked Nazia.

"How will you earn money, Sir?" asked Taheera.

"That's enough all of you! Why are you troubling him like this?" said Eva. "Let us not assume that he'll be expelled. Although, in all likelihood, he will be. And even if *is* expelled, I'm sure he'll find a job in other villages. You'll still be a teacher, won't you, Sir? Well, of course, you'll be! You can't be anything else! Whichever school takes you in, obviously it won't be as big as ours is, nor will the library be so generous. Who knows how the librarian will be? You probably won't find intelligent and dedicated children too, like us. But then again – we don't know anything for sure," Eva ended with a shrug. Ashwat Sir slumped on the chair, clutching his head in panic.

Just then, we heard Mahira Ma'am guffawing from her counter, heading towards us. It was the most normal laugh, but it seemed to instantly alleviate all our troubles. It was after a very long time that we'd heard such a laugh – a laugh which knew what happiness was and what it meant, a laugh made precious not because of its singularity but because it was naked with true contentment, a laugh used to itself.

"You are extremely naughty children!"

We tried to stifle our giggles but burst into an uproar when we glanced at Ashwat Sir's naive, hapless eyes.

"What? Why?" asked Ashwat Sir.

"They were fooling around with you! It *is* Saturday today and you haven't missed any classes," Mahira Ma'am said with as much sympathy as she could muster along with satisfying her glee. She was almost one of us – the children.

"What? You tricked me? Why do you hate me so much?" and he fell on the table, moaning, tired with relief.

"No, Sir. We wouldn't have done this had we hated you," replied Eric.

"Wow. Now, I wish you had hated me." It did not take him five seconds to join us in our hysterics after saying this. He was absolutely inept at staying angry at us for too long; this was his greatest weakness and the most forgivable too.

"Now let's come to the point – what are the six of you doing here on a Saturday morning?" asked Ashwat Sir.

"We need your help," I said, looking at Ashwat Sir and Mahira Ma'am.

"With?"

"With Eva, Nazia and Taheera's education." We gave them an elaborate account of how we had met Nazia and Taheera (we had lied to them about it prior to this, more out of solidarity towards the new relation than any sort of trust issue) and also the previous day's verdict by Eva's father.

"This is what you were worried about?" asked Ashwat Sir, his teasing eyes glistening with a comforting flicker.

"Yes…" I replied. I wasn't sure if it was an answer or another question.

"Since when did you start worrying?" That soothing flicker was still there.

"Shouldn't we be worried?" asked Vihaan.

"Of course not!" said Mahira Ma'am. She looked at Eva, Nazia and Taheera and said, "You have this entire library to study; you have Ashwat Sir and me to teach or explain to you anything you want; you have your friends who will report to you everything they learn at school every single day, and will also give you homework!" She moved her glance to Vihaan, Eric and me and said, "Won't you?"

"Yes! Yes! Yes, we will!" I said, jumping excitedly.

"We'll bring them our notes and repeat the exact words as we'd hear in class!" added Vihaan.

"And we'll give them lots of homework! More than they can manage!" said Eric, chuckling.

"So, there it is. Problem solved," said Ashwat sir, clapping his hands on his thighs, and got up. "The six of you have nothing to worry about as long as you are together."

"And as long as your Sir remains stubborn and you have access to so many books!" chimed in Ma'am, throwing her hands in the air and embracing the six of us in a warm, loving hug, her mouth wide in an ecstatic grin.

We were in the library. I was reading "Charlie and the Chocolate Factory," Nazia was busy devouring a world map, Eva had buried her head in a children's guide to chemistry; Eric and Vihaan were scrutinizing and discussing a bulky science encyclopaedia and Taheera was looking at a Tintin comic (yes, she was merely looking since she couldn't read, but the pictures always fascinated her) when Durga Di informed us about a heated meeting being conducted under the mango tree. Heated meetings were usual. There would be some passive-aggressive claims and threats, but people would soon compose themselves and put on a more rational façade, but this was only when the meeting was amongst villagers of the same village. That time, all three villages were attending it – together.

"What's the meeting about?" asked Mahira Ma'am.

"I don't know. I heard them arguing about the funds being given to the hospital and the school. I don't know anything beyond that."

"Should we go?" asked Eric.

"No. It wouldn't be safe," Ashwat Sir grimly replied. "We'll go," he said looking at Mahira Ma'am. "Let's bring along Dadu as well. Is he here?"

"Yes, yes. But he didn't seem very interested in attending the meeting."

"I'll talk to him," Mahira Ma'am assured.

She persuaded Dadu and the three of them went to the meeting. Durga Di stayed back to keep a check on our mischief.

(Mahira Ma'am's P.O.V.)

When we reached the rendezvous, we saw ten to twelve men towering over the seated villagers, yelling and vehemently gesturing at each other.

"There should be separate rooms and floors for people of all three villages in the hospital and school!"

"Yes! The children should not study together!"

"And we don't want the same hospital staff treating people from all three villages! We want separate staff!"

"Yes! What if a 'village A' patient manipulates the nurse or the doctor against a 'village C' patient? We need to ensure our safety!"

"What do you mean? Do you think people from 'village A' are monsters? How dare you say that?"

"I'll say whatever I want! Who are you to stop me?"

"Enough! These are all petty issues!" said the Head Sarpanch.

"Really? What did you want to discuss then?"

"I've received complaints from 'village B' that their place of worship is not as tall as that of the other two villages."

"This is bullshit! All three are equally tall!"

"No, they're not! We DO have a smaller structure. If you stand by the river, you can see the peak of places of worship of villages A and C, but not that of village B. We need to reconstruct it!"

"Have you lost your mind? We don't have money to relieve our debts and you are worried about reconstructing a damn place of worship?" retaliated a fellow, almost landless, villager B.

"You fool! Do you want to bring hell upon us? At least choose your words correctly before you refer to our place of worship!"

"I don't care! The only thing I care about is giving my family a good life! I don't care about the school getting divided! I simply want to educate all four of my children. I don't care if you want to divide the hospital and its staff! I just want to get my mother treated for cancer!"

"You must have done something wrong in your previous life," remarked a vain landlord from village A.

"That's easy for you to say. Don't worry. I'm sure you'll lead my life in your next life."

"What the hell do you mean by that?!"

"I couldn't have committed a bigger 'wrong' than the one you're committing in this life."

"What 'wrong' are you talking about, you bloody scumbag?"

"Why? Is there any higher 'wrong' than that of killing one's soul and then sucking it from others? You have all the money in the world, yet you extort profits from people who barely manage to survive with not a single coin in their pockets – people who cannot dream big, because even their dreams are filled with suffering, people for whom the only deliverance is death!"

"You are a mad man! I'll make sure nobody gives you any loans!"

"You're simply proving what I just said."

"We won't give you any loans even when you're on your deathbed!"

"We have again gone off-topic! Come back to dividing the hospital, the school rooms and the staff!"

"Yes! Ashwat, Adam and Mahira are here too!"

"Yes! Let's see what they have to say about this!"

"Adam, what do you think? Should we divide the hospital wards and staff into three groups?" asked the Head Sarpanch with exhausted, pleading eyes. He was eighty years old, but he wasn't as physically tired as he was mentally.

"No." Adam's curt reply drew violent gasps, probably because his single-word reply implied more conviction than a dimwit's thousand words speech ever could.

"What?"

"Why?"

"What the hell is this doctor saying?"

"Why, Adam?" asked the Head Sarpanch politely.

"Because I don't have the time nor the will to engage in pointless activities or submit to your useless demands."

"What is he saying?"

"What does he think of himself?"

"He thinks he knows more than us because he is a city boy!"

"Bloody doctor!"

"We don't need his permission!"

"Actually, you do. I own that hospital. And I have ensured to employ staff whom I don't feel like killing every next minute."

"These are his manners!"

"This is what he learnt in the city."

"This is why we shouldn't allow children to leave the village!"

"He has forgotten his manners and culture!"

"Is this how you treat the elders of your village?"

"Shame on you!"

"ENOUGH! Keep quiet everybody! Let the man speak. Adam, please be clearer and slightly less disrespectful."

"Okay. Every decision regarding the maintenance and administration of the hospital is made jointly. There are official meetings held for such purposes. The participants in these meetings are highly educated, qualified and experienced members, along with the villagers who provide their services to the hospital. Whenever a decision needs to be made, we take a poll. In my ten years as the owner of this hospital, I have never seen any glaring discrepancy among the opinions or viewpoints of my staff members. There have been discussions, arguments, debates, etc., – suggesting individual differences – but at the end of the day, the decision has been made democratically, taking into account the best interest of all the villagers. Let me also highlight the point that the villagers who attend these meetings are also given the opportunity to speak and submit their reasons since they are more connected to the grassroots level issues and therefore, demand the right to be consulted. This is the reason why our hospital is considered the best when compared to other hospitals in the area – although I would not have said this if I had looked at it singularly. What we lack is funding. We need more funds to improve our services and grant better and more holistic treatments. I understand that funds cannot be acquired from every single family in the three villages. It would be foolish to demand funds from people who can barely afford to fill their stomachs. But this isn't the case with landlords, moneylenders and priests. They would not have to skip a week's meals to be able to gather funds for the hospital. I want my hospital to grow. That is my only aim. The division of the hospital and its staff to comply with your communal dictates will only derail me from my mission, and I will not allow that." He had given his verdict. Nobody dared question it further.

"Alright. So, we have resolved the hospital aspect." The Head Sarpanch seemed much less fatigued. "Going on to the school… Ashwat, Mahira, what do you have to say about the villagers' demand?"

"There's another point, which Dr Adam left out," Ashwat began, "proportion – the proportion of patients to doctors/nurses and the proportion of students to teachers. We have more students from one particular village, but fewer teachers who belong to the village. What is the point if fifteen children get three teachers, but fifty children get two teachers? We have always maintained a fixed student-teacher ratio. I will not think of dividing the school and the teachers until you settle this."

"Even if this dimension of the problem is ever settled," I contributed, "I'll never be in favour of implementing a divisive stance. I don't want this generation to inherit your rotten mindsets. They should be able to read and explore without the slightest inhibition or barrier. So, please refrain from turning your children into another generation of hate-mongering monsters. Let them live as they want. Let them do what they want. Let them be whatever they want!"

13

THROUGH NAZIA'S VOICE

"Your Amma is dead."

It was Dadu. All six of us were sitting in our room. I don't know when he came and sat beside Taheera and me. Putting his palm on our heads, he said in a low, concerned voice, "I heard some of the villagers talking. They had come to my shop. Maybe it's time for the two of you to return…"

I could hear Taheera crying softly, but I wasn't crying. I couldn't cry. No matter how much I tried, I could not bring those tears to the brim; they were too heavy. I had gone into a state of paralysis. We were walking towards our house. I was walking, but my mind was numb. We were heading towards our village, but my mind was stuck in a dark chasm. I knew we were once again entering the devil's lair, but it did nothing to frighten me. I could hear a voice in my brain, shouting at me, "Your Amma is dead." No, it wasn't shouting as much as it was echoing and amplifying with each successive echo, as if the voice wanted me to shatter in the middle of the road like a rock constantly beaten by water. But I took no notice of it and marched on. I could hear my heart pounding against my chest as we drew nearer our house. The numbness seemed to be spreading through the length and breadth of my body like the roots of a weed unfurling its tentacles to conquer the soil. I had long forgotten that I was walking, but hauling the entire weight of my body forward.

"Nazia! Wait. We are here," Taheera's voice sounded much more stable. We had crossed the village entryway and reached our house.

I stopped and turned my head towards our house. The door was locked.

"Why is the door locked?" I asked, clutching the shirt of the first person I saw passing us by.

"Aren't you the girls who ran away months back? So now you've returned…"

"Answer the question! Why is the door locked?! Where IS everybody?"

"Wow. Your father really should have broken your legs. They had gone to the hospital," he replied nonchalantly.

After this encounter, we ran. We ran as fast as our legs and the wind could allow us. I was out of my paralytic shock. Anybody willing to fight me was most welcome. But I wanted to be with Amma. I wanted to know what had happened to her. I wanted to know why it could not be avoided. I wanted to know why we had been left bereft of the only person we loved and cared for in that wretched hell for a family.

We ran towards the reception as soon as we reached the hospital and enquired about Amma. Instead, we were welcomed by our father.

"Oho! Welcome back! My lovely daughters!"

"Where is Amma? What happened to her?" I asked impatiently.

"She is dead. Thank you for coming back though."

"No, you're lying. You're a dirty, filthy liar!" Taheera yelled at him.

"Shut up, idiot girl! You decide to show your faces after months, and then have the audacity to misbehave with your father? It's good that your mother died; she was of no use even when she was alive. She couldn't even teach her daughters to stay within their limits."

"Don't talk about Amma from your nasty mouth," I threatened him.

"Oh? Or else what? What will you do? WHAT WILL YOU DO?" He seized our arms and pulling both of us towards him, screamed the last question on our faces.

"WHAT ARE YOU DOING?" It was Dr Adam. He didn't raise his voice, but his eyes were enough to lay bare his rage. "Leave the girls! You are in a hospital. Are you not aware of that? There are people here who are SICK!" His eyes were most capable of reducing our father's rage to a cat's purr. There was repulsion of the purest form in them. When he looked at us, although his eyes were burning with fury, there was a trace of tenderness too which overpowered his fury; not only because we had been robbed of our mother, but more so because we had been left on Earth with a demon.

"Will YOU tell us what happened to Amma?" I demanded.

"She had an accident." I could see clouds of guilt hovering over his face.

"And?" Taheera persisted.

"How? Where? When? Give us the details!" I emphasized.

"I can't." Off he went, after one last lingering glare at our father.

We followed him to his office, begging and imploring him to let us in on the exact reason.

"Alright!" he exclaimed, exasperated. "Maybe it's well that you should know what happened to her. It's your right. But Taheera, I can't tell you about it."

"Why not?" Her eyes were watery.

"You have to trust me on this. Please. Your sister will tell you in a few years. But this isn't something that I should be telling you. Will you please trust me? Eva, can you take her outside with you?"

"Sure, Dr Adam." Eva took her outside, wiping her tears off and consoling her.

"Nazia, please have a seat."

My throat was drying up and I was feeling weak in the knees. Having seated myself on the edge of the chair, I managed to say to him, "Tell me." I could feel myself losing control, standing on the coast of a vast, magnificent ocean, combating the urge to immerse myself in it – whether to forget myself in its grandeur and resplendence or to discover its darkest secrets, I didn't know.

"I believe that your father forced himself on your mother."

"What do you mean?"

"I mean that he probably raped her. Violently. She was pregnant too."

We had buried her. The rituals were done. The priest was gone. Our cousin, who had been given the job of chaperoning us back to our village, was waiting for us in the distance. But there was something which forbade me to move – which kept me there fixated, staring at her gravestone. I felt a sudden constriction in my throat, like two ends of a thin string stretching themselves and the self-woven knot tighter and tighter, waiting for it to break.

Ultimately, it broke and I collapsed on the ground, crying vehemently, and the more I cried, the harder I found it to stop. The last time I had seen her face was six months back when she had discreetly helped us escape. If only I had taken another look at her, if only I had hugged her once more, if only I had felt her kiss on my forehead once more, if only I COULD SEE HER ONCE MORE.

"Nazia." I felt a hand on my left shoulder. I wiped my tears and tried to look at the person standing behind me through my red, moist eyes.

It did not take me by surprise that Tamanna, Vihaan, Eva and Eric had come to the cemetery. I had grown accustomed to their care, their constant interrogations of whether we had slept comfortably or not, or if we required anything else for our small room in the school; if the room required cleaning or if we needed help with it; whether or not I had finished reading a book, or if Taheera had been practising her lessons. Being shocked at their visit would have been an insult to the very essence of our friendship.

I looked up at them – Tamanna, Eva, Eric and Vihaan – and before I could return to Tamanna, she embraced me and Taheera in a tight hug. Eva, Vihaan and Eric followed suit. I was still crying, but the burden had been shared.

"Who were those children?" our cousin later asked me while we were leaving the cemetery.

"My family."

Taheera clutched my hand, looked him in the eye, and said, "Our family".

14

1983 – AN ENCOUNTER

I was three years old when I had my first encounter with the word *"dange"* (riots) – literally and theoretically. Ever since, the sole feeling this word has evoked in me is paramount hatred, even before I knew what the feeling meant. I couldn't ascertain anything that day, but today, when I look back, everything is as crystal clear as though it were happening right in front of me – like a movie which gives you the utmost pain, and yet, doesn't allow you to close your eyes for a second, as if the movie were meant to be for atonement.

It began with Durga Di frantically trying to wake me up but resorting to carrying me in her arms in the end. I was annoyed with her for disrupting my pretty slumber and incessantly tried to jump out of her arms. It did not take me long to break free, and as I strained my neck to glare at her, the face I saw can be repainted hundreds of times, and it still won't do justice. Considering she's six years older than me, she was nine back then, and you'll come across very few nine-year-old children who are afraid of life. Durga Di was one of them. The fear I was used to seeing on her face – since I gained the ability of comprehension and retention – was veiled, hiding in the nooks of her eyebrows and crooks of her eyes, and speckled like dust on her forehead. But THAT day, the fear had scaled newer and unidentified levels of profundity. She was crimson with sweat and panic, her hair running everywhere, her salwar kameez drenched, and her feet bleeding. She wasn't wearing any shoes. She knelt down, took me by my hand and said through jittering teeth, "You will behave yourself! Don't you dare try to wriggle out! Or else…" I wonder at times what she would have done had I tried to wriggle my way out again. But I knew better. My love and respect for her were too immense to not be able to discern that something had gone terribly haywire.

She picked me up on her shoulder and fled the house.

"What's *appning*?" I cried. I had sensed the tension on her face. I could feel it in the air too.

"Nothing. Just keep quiet." There was never any question about how hard she tried to console me – a three-year-old – but I had already seen her face! Her voice was stable, but her countenance, as she had glared down at me defied all her future attempts to reassure me. I had only a vague idea of where we were headed. I was three and I had only just begun exploring the villages. Moreover, I was too preoccupied with dissecting our environment – some of the rooftops were blazing as if the sun had shot fire at them; some people were chasing others with violent torches or sleek, sharp knives; some of the men were running with their parents perched on their shoulders, but some had also locked their houses and left their old parents thudding on the door and the window; the women were carrying either some luggage or their children. I distinctly remember two women – both of whom had passed us in pursuit of a shelter. The former was carrying three children – one on her neck, and two on her arms. She had lost control of her saree. In the next five seconds, she evaded tripping on her saree, leaving her torn blouse and petticoat and purple bruises for the world to gawk at. The latter was actually a girl, not much older than Durga Di, but much more distressed. It wasn't only the environment that accounted for her distress, but probably also the trail of blood she was leaving behind as she ran with her mother. I remember probing her from head to toe in search of an injury, but there was none.

I was revived from my trance when I heard a splash underneath us. Durga Di was still running, but her left foot was suddenly very red.

"Di! What happened to your leg?!" I cried.

"I didn't see the puddle."

"But puddles are muddy! Or sometimes watery! And water is not red! Is it?"

"No, it isn't."

"Then why is your leg red?" I had tears in my eyes.

"It was a puddle of blood. There was a man lying beside it. Or a woman. I couldn't see properly."

"Why?"

"There was too much blood on the face." I clutched her tighter. I was too afraid to glance anywhere else. So, I closed my eyes and buried my face in her moist, sweaty hair.

When I reopened my eyes, I could see tall, massive buildings around me. "What are these, Di?" I asked since I had never seen anything made of something other than mud and straw or hay.

"These are buildings."

"What?"

"BIL – DINGS," she distinctly pronounced the word.

"PIL – DIGS. Pildigs."

"Close."

"But what are they made of? They don't seem to be mud or hay."

"They are made of cement, bricks and glass."

"SI – MET, PRIKS and GLAASS. Is that right?"

"No. But you'll learn. Don't worry."

"Okay. But why are we here?"

"We are safe here."

"From?"

"From the rioters."

"The what?"

"Rioters. People who engage in and create riots. *Dange.*"

"Di! These are too many new words for one day!"

"It's okay. You need not know their meanings or pronunciations today. You'll soon know it."

"Whatever it is, I don't like it."

"The word?"

"Yes."

After a while, I asked, "Where is everybody else?"

"In that little shop, there."

"Already? How did they reach so early? They weren't in the house when you woke me!"

"They had left before us."

"Why? Why didn't they take us?"

"There was no point." I couldn't understand her answers, yet I persisted, "Why didn't Ma wait for us?"

"He didn't let her." I knew *who* the 'he' was, and *how* he didn't 'let her.'

We returned to our village two weeks later. Naveen was clutching Ma's saree with one hand, and Durga Di's frock with the other. *'Dainty darling,'* I thought (I had heard Rahul Bhaiya address Durga Di this way). Durga Di was holding my hand more tightly than I was holding hers and was also carrying a bag with the other.

When we crossed the river, I felt a sudden cold air hit me on the face, despite the sun being extremely exuberant that morning. But there are limits to what a three-year-old brain can discern. It took me seven years and a reunion to realise what the cold air was, and what it signified.

The instant I saw Dadu opening and organising his little shop, I wrenched my hand away and ran to him.

"Dadu!" I exulted. He knelt down and hugged me. It was not the usual kind of hug, the one which testified his affection for me. It was something else, like one seeking solace and comfort, and having finally found it in the slender frame of a three-year-old girl. We remained in that position until I heard a soft sob from him.

"Dadu? Are you crying?" Peering into his moist eyes, I couldn't control my tears either. I was too attached to him. "Dadu, why are you crying?"

"It's nothing, Tamanna. I'm just really happy to see you and Durga back. And everybody else too," he replied wiping his eyes. By this time, my family had also reached Dadu's shop.

"Tamanna, go to your sister. I have to talk to Dadu," my father commanded.

"No! Dadu is sad! I'll stay with him!" I retaliated.

"Did you not hear what I said?" he asked pressing my arms.

"Now, now. She's just a child," Dadu intervened, pulling his hand and my arm away. "Tamanna, why don't you and Durga go to my shop and pick out some toffees? I'll give you three for free, and the fourth toffee onwards, I'll charge you a kiss on both cheeks. Deal?" Dadu said, grinning.

"DEAL!" I yelled with exultation.

I obeyed Dadu and went to his shop, but I couldn't help overhearing the conversation between my father and Dadu.

"Dadu, where is *Dadi*? Have you sent her somewhere?"

"I never *sent* her anywhere. She went whenever and wherever she wished. But this time, it was against her wish."

"What? What happened to her?"

"The rioters. They got her."

"WHAT? How the *hell* is that possible?"

"*Shhh*! Don't shout! They didn't get her purposely."

"What happened exactly?"

"They wanted to destroy the school, but she stood in front of the door and told them to go away. They warned her with their knives, but she didn't stir. They pushed her aside, but she came back. She was trying to pull them back, but they were stubborn too. One of the men accidentally thrust his knife inside her."

"Where were you all this while?"

"I had heard a shriek amongst the crops and had gone to check that."

"And who told you about Dadi?"

"The man confessed to me a week back."

"Who's shriek was it?" asked my grandfather who had joined their conversation.

"A small girl's."

I was greeted with a peculiar unfamiliarity when I entered our village. Everybody was running. Towards? I haven't been able to discern. From? From whatever it was that was chasing them. The monstrous riot had ended, but I could still see its ghost in their eyes. It was still living in them, in their souls, minds and memory. The people somehow seemed trapped in a stagnant quicksand – the riot had ensnared them and was exhausting them internally. They couldn't come out of it no matter how hard they tried to shove it into the depths of their memory. For a long, long time, they remained entrapped there.

I hadn't finished glancing around when we stopped in front of a black, dilapidated "something." I didn't know what else to call it.

"We'll have to rebuild it," our father mumbled.

"But why? What is this thing? Where is our house?" I inquired.

"Don't you think you ask too many questions for your age?"

"That's our house. They've burnt it," said Rahul Bhaiya.

"Who burnt it?" No, I never stopped asking questions.

"The rioters."

"But why did they burn our house? What had we done?"

"Exactly. They shouldn't have burnt the house. They should have burnt YOU so that we wouldn't have to answer all your stupid questions!" our father bellowed at me.

"Tamanna, *shhhh!*" shushed Durga Di as she pulled me closer to her.

15

AN ESCAPE AND A TRUTH

Exactly six years after my first encounter, it was Nazia's ninth birthday. We hadn't seen her and Taheera for two months because their father had arrested their social activities, and for that matter, any pleasurable activity. They were conferred with numerous variants of thrashing for not revealing their hiding place. So, the school storeroom was still secure. Dadu was still secure. We were still secure. But at the price of our two friends. Their lives were hanging by a thread. Again. But fortunately for their grandfather, he paused the beastly lunacy of his son while the two girls were on the verge of losing that last ounce of breath from their bodies. It will always remain a mystery to me why he never intervened in the initial seconds of his son's acts of savagery. But even a veiled demon can sometimes echo the actions of an angel. In the sisters' case, the obscurity of the Angel and the Demon's actions made it difficult to discern their roles – one beat his daughters till they were as much out of breath as he out of his senses, and the other pulled them back each time they attempted to leave this relentlessly harrowing place.

Eva, Eric, Vihaan and I had been planning Nazia's birthday for a month. Our primary gift to her was escape. We were more enthusiastic about rescuing her from that place than actually celebrating her birthday. For thirty days, we tracked their family members' schedules. The only window available to us was four o'clock in the morning, and that was the hour around which we formulated and executed our plans. Their father came back to the house at the most by three-thirty in the morning, and their grandmother awoke at five, followed by their grandfather at six.

We had stationed Eric outside their village, hiding behind a bush. Eva was perched on the mango tree to keep a lookout and because she had the sharpest eyes among us. In case of any imminent danger, she simply had to send out a *cuckoo*, which would be reciprocated by Eric to me and Vihaan – the ones in the forefront of the battlefield.

Their house had an unused door at one of the extreme corners. It was badly rusted but had been taken care of by us in the past month. The four of us would alternately go there in disguise, and properly oil the hinges. Getting caught would have been a largely improbable scenario because their house shared the perimeter with the adjacent forest, and that was the escape route we had planned for them – running along the perimeter until we reached the school, completely bypassing the village and the overly-enthusiastic eyes of the villagers.

When Vihaan and I reached their house, we decided to move from the back end of the house; the door was more easily accessible too. Slowly and carefully, avoiding even the feeblest sound, we unlocked the latch. Just as steadily, we opened the door too. While Vihaan kept guard outside, I tiptoed inside, giving myself time to adjust to the darkness. Before moving forward, I looked around in all directions to familiarise myself with the surroundings and to not trip over something and create a noise. Once I had figured out a rough layout of their house, I proceeded to glance into one of the rooms and found their father peacefully snoring away in his sleep. There was another room leading via his, that required me to enter his room before continuing my search for the sisters. Once again, I took a preview of his room before venturing inside so as to avoid any accidents. Holding my slippers in my hand and barely making any sound, I entered. I took a right turn, keeping as close to the wall as possible, and peeked inside the next room. I had found them. I scampered towards them and leaning down, woke them up.

"Nazia! Taheera! Wake up! And *shh*! Don't make any noise. Come with me." Their father's erratic outbursts and the proclivity to give in to his random impulses had made both the sisters hyper-vigilant, even in their sleep. Both of them were wide awake within a few seconds.

I led them outside and quietly closed the door behind me. Everything had gone according to the plan; completely smooth; except that one moment when I saw them in the morning light and went into a trance – their swollen, distorted faces, crimson eyes, purple and red blemishes on the limbs, the scattered cuts trying to heal, short, dishevelled hair, their rough skin peeking through the holes in their dresses.

"Tamanna!" Vihaan nudged me. "Let's go!"

A few months later, all of us were napping in the shadow of the mango tree when…

"Nazia?" It was Faham, their neighbour's son.

"Faham? Hello. What are you doing here?"

"I have come to tell you about your mother."

"What about her?"

"I know how she died." By then, everyone was up.

"Tell me."

"Your mother had been pregnant in the course of her last six months. The night before her death, your father had broken up with his mistress. When he returned home…"

"House," Nazia interrupted.

"When he returned, he saw Auntie crying because she had been chided by your grandmother a few minutes back, and he poured all his frustration out on her. He slapped her, threw dishes at her – most of which she precariously dodged – and dragged her to their room. The next thing I heard was a shrill scream from your house. I pleaded with my father to go and check, but he wouldn't budge and instead locked me in my room. I woke up in the morning to your father's vainglorious narration to my father about how he tore off her clothes, pressed her frontward against the wall and went on to "relieve" himself; then threw her – this time mercifully on the bed – and further "relieved" himself. When, with whatever little ounce of strength she had left in her, she pushed him and attempted for the door, he crawled towards her, seized and pulled her leg, such that she fell on her stomach frontward. He hauled her up to bring her face-to-face with him and the agony that he saw on her face then, and in the fifteen minutes hence, brought him "joy he had never experienced before." To quote him exactly, he left the room when he was truly and utterly satisfied. Your grandmother went to the room in the morning to check why Auntie had not begun with her morning chores when she found something blocking the door. Auntie was lying there, in a pool of her own blood, still; naked; dead. She wrapped her up in one of her clothes and called your grandfather to take her to the hospital. The doctors could do nothing. She was brought dead."

16

THE MARRIAGE

Approximately five months after Nazia's birthday was Durga Di and Rihan Bhaiya's wedding. The five months which led up to their wedding were probably the most normal months one could ever imagine – five months fraught with abuses, arguments escalating to vanishing sanity, entreaties resulting in temper upheavals, and the usual beating, crying, humiliating, insulting, so on and so forth.

Rihan Bhaiya protested to the alliance because he wanted to build a career for himself prior to a marriage, and because he barely knew her. Durga Di was opposed because she barely knew him either (Durga Di had never pondered over her career, and even if she had, she'd long forgotten about it). But somehow, it seemed to be more important for our parents to unload a burden, than for the to-be in-laws to get their elder son married. For the latter, she was merely a good prospect. For the former, he was the best and the last prospect – last, because our father had professed his intention to disencumber this 'responsibility' in the instance of an unsuccessful agreement.

A few days prior to the wedding, I asked Durga Di, "Di, why do you not want to marry Rihan Bhaiya? I like him."

"Do you know when Ma got married?" Durga Di counter questioned.

"No."

"She was eleven."

"Really? And what age was Papa?"

"Thirty."

"WHAT? Couldn't they find someone their own age?"

"They could. They didn't."

"Why?"

"Because a man can marry at any age. It doesn't make much of a difference. But a girl cannot. Once she passes a certain age and is still unmarried, she is no more considered pure or fit or qualified enough."

"And what is that 'certain age?'"

"I don't know. But it shouldn't be too late from puberty."

"What's *poobuty*?"

"You'll know it later."

From my experience of my sister's wedding preparations, I can safely infer that the bride and the bridegroom had absolutely no contribution in their own ceremony, save for the brief, but frequent intervals, in which they reminded everyone how utterly averse they were to this marriage alliance. There was nothing novel in these reminders – nothing which had not been said before, yelled before or endured before. But one could not call it repetitive. A repetition is mundane. Their reminders weren't repetitive because they were attestations of their defiance of a life forced upon them. They weren't repetitive because with each passing day, and each passing hour, the shadow of the realisation that they would soon lose their battle, and inherit a life and relationship they had come to abhor, seemed to loom larger and darker on them. Vihaan and I too, weren't particularly enjoying the show. Though merely nine years old, we could understand what that marriage symbolised, and somewhat gauge Rihan Bhaiya's and Durga Di's anguish.

I hadn't paid much heed to the ceremonies and rituals which led up to the wedding. They were all a farce, a pomp show, a façade to mask our destitution. It amazed me that we could even afford that façade. Therefore, I can't recollect the details of those rituals. What I do remember is the misery on the faces of the bride and the groom. It was so palpable, and yet, nobody seemed to take notice of it. Was that how the bride and the groom were supposed to be? Was it normal? Was the indifference of the guests justified? If yes, then why? If not, then why was it tolerated? Why were the guests indifferent? Was it intentional, or unintentional? If it was intentional, what reason could have driven them to be so agonisingly cruel? If it was unintentional, what life circumstance had robbed them of their sensitivity?

Contrary to the pre-wedding rituals, the wedding day is still very clearly etched in my memory. When THE day came, Durga Di was still adamant, although passively. She hadn't slept the previous night, she hadn't eaten anything in the morning, and when told to get ready by Papa, she simply went to our room, picked up a book, sat on the floor, and started reading. This was not received very humbly or graciously by Papa. He twice told Durga Di to obey – his fury making leaps and bounds with each syllable. The second time she chose to take no notice of him, Durga Di was greeted by his flying chappal. It hit her forehead leaving a reddish-purple spot on it. Grandmother chastised Papa for behaving this way on Durga Di's wedding day, "Where did you lose your brain? Look at her forehead! See what you have done! What if they refuse her for the marriage? What will we do then? Idiot boy."

"Don't even think about it!" he bellowed at his mother. "If she doesn't get married today, she will not see tomorrow's dawn. And I mean it." He glared at Durga Di to re-emphasize his resolution and left the room. Our grandmother left too, but Ma stayed back.

"Please do it, Durga," Ma begged. "I know you don't want to. But that is seldom a privilege granted to us."

"What privilege, Ma?" Durga Di asked.

"The privilege to decide and choose for ourselves. The privilege to say 'no.'"

"It is not a privilege, Ma!" Turning to me, she said, "Do you see what the problem is? Do you understand now? The actual problem? The problem isn't only how our fathers, brothers and grandfathers treat us. The larger – and often resistant to immediate comprehension – problem lies in how we treat ourselves!"

Durga Di returned to Ma and said, "Choosing not to live a life of degradation and constraint is not a privilege, Ma! It is a basic right! Being able to say 'no,' with its implication understood in entirety by the person it is addressed to is a basic right! MY right! Deciding whether or not I want to be tied to a person for the rest of my life IS MY RIGHT! Don't call it a privilege, Ma. Please don't. You are reducing us to brainless dimwits who have no dignity and no identity, and toil to derive these from the outside world – a world which has always been relentless in its pursuit to squash and crumble us. I know who I am, I know how and from where I want to derive my dignity, and I know that I am not going to submit to Papa this time." Durga Di was implacable.

"Durga, I don't care about who you think you are. I don't care about your idealism. What I do care about is that if you don't marry Rihan today, your father will not blink an eyelid before killing you. So, let me offer you a better negotiation – either you marry Rihan today, or I will kill myself."

"Ma!" we cried in unison.

"That is my final word." With that, she walked out.

"Do you think she meant that?" I asked Durga Di, still aghast that Ma would even think of doing something like this.

"I don't know." Durga Di's incredulity seemed bigger than mine. "But can we take the chance?"

I looked at Durga Di and back again at the door, and realised her implicit declaration, the selflessness of her sacrifice and the immensity of her courage. I murmured a half-hearted reply, "No."

Durga Di's adornment commenced half an hour later. This task, of rendering my sister the least bit presentable, and saving the family from disgrace, was assumed by our grandmother. I had been appointed the task of helping Ma in the kitchen. My brothers were helping my father and grandfather with the more laborious and backbreaking work. The ceremony was to take place in the 'abode of God.' We boarded a *tonga* at thirty-five minutes past seven. It was being hurled by a man who seemed to be my father's age, but without any ounce of flesh in his body. His forehead had acquired natural furls, and his puckered eyebrows had probably found peace in the shade of those furls. His muscles constricted at the slightest movement of his limbs, as though tired of this seemingly endless enslavement. His eyes betrayed his chagrin for living a life pitied even by the sinners of infernal hell. The sinners had their sins to support their predicament. What did he have to support his predicament – the sin of existence?

I was separated from my reverie by the noisy chatter and thrill of the crowd gathered at the stairs of the wedding venue. Each and every individual there had adorned the best clothing possible. Not only were the rituals farcical (as I mentioned before), but the spectacle there too, was a performance, meant only to impress and flaunt. I learned the perfect word for that image I had so minutely imprinted on my memory a few months hence – OSTENTATIOUS.

If I were to disintegrate that view into smaller and finer details, this is how it would go…

The women were huddled on one side, and the men clustered a little further away from their wives. Behind them was the place of worship exclusive to our village. It had taken my grandfather innumerable pains to arrange the wedding there. It would have been easier if my father had not been known as a local nuisance. But my grandfather too had powers I was incapable of noticing at the tender age of eight. He was incredibly persuasive, had mastered the skill of playing the victim card, and was known – famously or infamously – as a sycophant.

All these qualities successfully placated our priest into lending us the place of worship for a few hours on the date of 28 February 1989 at 8:30 a.m. It was a particularly sunny day, as I remember looking up at the sky, searching for clouds and finding none. '*The sun is grinning with its glistening, shiny teeth, mocking the insanity of the whole circumstance, while the clouds have decided to flee the situation altogether. Why? Are they afraid it will be too sad and pathetic to behold? Are they afraid it will pierce them as bitterly as a salty drop of tear pierces an open, raw wound? Or are they afraid it will drive them to tears? But haven't they been eternally considered to be the tear-bearers?*'

When my gaze returned to our guests, I could not identify them. These were people I had grown up seeing almost every day. But that day, at that moment, I could not recognize a single one of them. Everyone was so *pleasant* – not only in their countenance but also in their temperament. The women were chatting and giggling, while their male counterparts could be seen laughing boisterously. All of them had decked up impeccably for the special day. I still remember some of the conversations I heard –

"Hadn't your husband beaten you a couple of days back? I cannot see any bruise!"

"Nor can I!"

"He had! But my brother's friend's sister lives in the city, and she sent me an expensive make-up kit as a present on my birthday last year!"

"A make-up kit! How did your in-laws allow you to keep that?"

"They don't even know about it! That's the best part!"

"But didn't they enquire about the bruises?"

"They did. But my reply was simple – Do you want your daughter-in-law to look beautiful today amongst fifty people, or not? That silenced them."

And all of them erupted laughing. What were they laughing at? At their pitiable life, which disallowed them to own even a make-up kit, or at their own acknowledgement of this pitiable life – an acknowledgement which was subconsciously propelling them into devising ways that would help them avoid accepting the futility of an existence marked by voluntary subservience.

I tried wandering towards the men's huddle to overhear their conversation. This is how that went…

"So, my wife came to me the other day, asking for ten rupees. I asked her why. And she says that she wants to buy a new set of bangles because she broke the current ones in the kitchen. And I tell her, 'Darling, why don't you tell your parents to return the loan they had taken from me five years back for your sister's marriage, and then I will think about giving you the ten rupees.'" Apparently, this was a hilarious incident.

"Your wife has a sister too? Poor father…"

"Not 'a' sister! She has three more sisters! My wife is the oldest one."

"Three more?"

"That's really sad."

"God bless the father…"

"Truly. They had to get her younger sister married – the one for whom I gave the loan – as soon as they got to know that she was found getting overly friendly with another girl her age. If you know what I mean…" This drew sharp breaths from everyone. He was drawn aside by a woman – presumably, his wife – at this point.

"That was a family secret! Why did you tell it to them?" the woman enquired.

"It wasn't a family secret when your sister had to be married off in the span of less than a week. And these are my friends. I can tell them whatever I wish to. Who are you to stop me?"

"Drop the matter. Talk about anything else but this!"

"And who are *you* to command *me*? If you don't want me to humiliate you in public, shut up and go back to your gossip huddle."

"As if yours isn't a gossip huddle…" she muttered as she walked away, leaving her husband glaring at her.

The man had not yet returned to his group when I heard my name yelled out by our father. The priest had given the orders to bring the bride and I had to help her disembark the tonga. Her face was veiled, so I could not see her expression, and so, I cannot describe it even now. But I don't think it needs any description. Considering the events that preceded the wedding, imagining her face at that moment is not exactly a herculean task.

While I escorted her, I could hear all sorts of comments.

"She looks beautiful, doesn't she?"

"She does! Look how gracefully she is walking!"

"She is definitely lucky!"

"True! Rihan is such a good boy!"

"She is going into a good household."

"I hope she is as skilled as she is beautiful."

"True. What use is her beauty otherwise?"

"What is *she* otherwise."

"Even if she isn't, she will learn. I am actually worried about the younger one."

"Their youngest girl?"

"Yes."

"What about her?"

"Don't you know? She is a brat! Always running around wild, playing with Rihan's brother and with those children of the other villages."

"She does?"

"Oh, yes! Always! The six of them are always together. God knows doing what not."

"I've heard Dadu speak very fondly of these children."

"He speaks fondly of everyone."

"No, you don't understand. His eyes light up the minute he starts talking about these six. And there's no stopping him once he starts on this topic. He rambles on forever!"

"Dadu is a good man. But he can be a bit naïve sometimes."

"Aren't you judging them a bit too harshly?"

"No, I'm not! She can find girls her age in this village itself to play with! But playing with boys and children of other villages… What is the need? You tell me."

"I don't know…"

I pretended to be deaf to all these observations. But the truth was, I was infuriated. It is a popular conception – or misconception – that children don't "understand things." This belief, though ill-founded and narrow, validates any and every action or speech of theirs which could otherwise have an impact. I sometimes think that children feel things more deeply than even adults. This is more so, because adults have the maturity to attend to certain thoughts or words, and conversely, not to attend to other more painful thoughts or words. But can this filter or decision-making ability be expected to be fully developed in the mind of an eight-year-old? No. They feel whatever their hearts lead them to feel to whatever extent possible. They haven't yet learnt the art of selective attention; only, it wasn't really an art in those times. It had to be developed as a coping mechanism, which I refused. Had I not done so, I would not have been writing this book today.

The ceremony commenced eventually, and all the guests gathered around the bride and the bridegroom. I retreated at the back – behind all the people – with those words still echoing in my ears. There, I met Vihaan. He too didn't look particularly happy.

"What happened to you? Why are you so dejected?" I inquired.

"This is all a sham," he replied in a monotone.

"What is?"

"This wedding. This marriage."

"Why do you say so?"

"My brother wants to live in the city and get a job there. He is only a school graduate, so he is not very hopeful. But he still wants to try. And if time and money permit, he might even pursue college."

"Really? That's amazing!"

"Wait till you hear the next part. Our parents have no objection to him earning a living in the city. They just wanted someone to take care of him while he toils."

"Take care of him? He is not crippled! And if it's really that difficult, he can always hire a servant."

"He won't have to…now."

"What do you mean?"

"He won't have to hire a servant. Your sister will be there to 'take care' of him."

I stared at him in utter disbelief for a few seconds, before venturing to ask, "Is that why this marriage is happening? So that Durga Di will *serve* Rihan Bhaiya?"

"In a way, yes. That's another reason why he did not want to get married."

The next few minutes passed in silence, breached only by the ritual chants. Vihaan was too preoccupied with scorning at the occurrence that he perceived to be a great "sham," and I was too overwhelmed by the information Vihaan had just imparted me. My sister's life was in the making of a new chapter, a new phase; but instead of bringing with it experiences which could be excitedly anticipated, it was basking in the stench of familial remorse, marital disgrace and sheer human indignity.

The remainder of the day passed as eventless as the skirmishes which had led up to it. That evening, I returned to a house quite alien to me. Apart from Durga Di, I did not particularly share a bond with anyone, except partly with our mother. Staying in that house, sleeping in that room, on that mattress, without Durga Di by my side, seemed unnatural. I had a restless sleep that night, and usually, on such nights, Durga Di would softly caress my hair till I dozed off with my forehead lightly touching against hers. But she wasn't there that night. In the end, when I found nothing to calm my mind, I decided to cry myself to sleep.

The dawn brought with it news of Durga Di's first night in a new household, amongst new people. All of us, except Vihaan, were sitting under the shade of our sanctum, our mango tree, when we saw him approach us. His face bore the same dejection that I had seen the previous day, only now it was coupled with desperation and disappointment. Let this be known that Vihaan never let his emotions reflect on his face and could be said to epitomise tremendous equanimity even in the direst of circumstances. But there is always a fine line, which, if crossed, will break the carefully held equanimity; and if it ever so happens, that the resting lion decides to forsake its soporific state, what form it will thus conjure is unpredictable and to some extent, unimaginable. This was one of those instances.

"You don't look good. What happened?" Eva asked.

"How is Durga Di?" Call it my self-centredness, but at that moment, I was more concerned about my sister than my friend.

"She is fine," Vihaan replied assuredly.

"And you?" urged Nazia.

"Not so fine, probably?" Eric answered on his behalf, receiving a nudge and a chastising glare from Eva.

"Bhaiya is planning to leave for the city next week."

"So?"

"He wants *me* to accompany him and Durga Didi."

"What?" I exclaimed.

"But it would be temporary, right?" Taheera interjected.

"No. Permanent."

We stared at each other, aghast. What if the sun, whose vibrance you had come to rely upon, whose brilliance you were fortunate enough to witness each day, whose charm and solicitude were responsible for devouring many a pall, suddenly, one day, failed to rise? It will be cold, chilly; and the mere thought of it makes you shudder.

"I think it'll be good for you, Vihaan," said Eva after much consideration.

"What?"

"Going to the city."

"Why?"

"For starters, you'll be out of this hell," answered Eric.

"You'll be in a much more secure and much less abusive environment," added Nazia.

"You'll be surrounded by better schools and hospitals," said Eva.

"You'll probably meet more like-minded people," I furthered.

"What about you? My friends?" countered Vihaan, agitated.

"You'll make new friends," replied Taheera.

"And we'll sneak out to come and meet you too!" smirked Eric.

"I won't get better teachers than Mahira Ma'am and Ashwat Sir."

"You might. One can't be sure," Eva tried to reassure. Vihaan stared at Eva, probably to convince himself that her words were not meant as ridicule or said blithely. The desperation which I had earlier detected on his face now effaced all other emotions. But there was also a trace of resolution – a resolution to not give in to the situation, a defiance to a life being forced upon him. He jolted his head to stare at the ground, and soon checked himself and what his face was involuntarily betraying. The equanimity returned, though only for a while.

"What are you thinking?" I asked when I felt certain that he had collected himself enough to be able to answer without giving way to that well I had sensed saturating beneath his eyes when he had looked at Eva.

"What I am sure of."

"What are you sure of?"

"That I don't want to go."

"What?"

"He has finally lost his mind."

"Mad. Absolutely mad."

"God save him."

"Why and how are you so sure, Vihaan?" I asked him softly, holding his hand.

"Because I don't want to leave my friends! I don't want to leave YOU! I cannot! You've been my family! I never knew what 'family' or 'friendship' meant till I met all of you; especially Tamanna - my first friend ever. I still remember the day when I first saw you. We had visited your place to see Durga Di, and you arrived after us. You were so brusque and precise when my mother interrogated you, that was the moment when I felt a sense of kindred to you. I thought, 'Now she is a girl who cannot, does not, and will not submit to pretension or feign respect. I wish Ma had a daughter like her. It would have been so fun to watch Ma agitated because of her. If only we could be friends! We would probably get along very well!' And then we did become friends! And we got along extremely well! You introduced me to Eva and Eric. Not long after, we met Nazia and Taheera. Had I not met you that day, my life today would have been unimaginable, and in all likelihood, unbearable too. I don't know what or whom I would have called my family if it were not for the five of you, because I don't feel any familial affection towards my parents! I don't know if that's wrong on my part, or if it's only what they deserve, but it is what it is."

He paused to gather himself, and continued, "I can endure anything – my parents' abuse, reproaches, humiliations, separation from my brother…anything! The only thing that's intolerable to me is living as though my life were not mine, but a burden, because I won't have my friends around me – my only true family. Our lives are so entwined, it's impossible to remove one single thread from this mesh!"

"Vihaan, nobody is removing any thread. Nobody can. Do you know why? Because we are not threads. We are a whole, a 'completeness.' If you remove a part of this whole, it will not remain the same. It will not remain the 'completeness' that it is supposed to be. But right now, you're being impractical. You're being given an opportunity for a fresh beginning, and you're denying that. You can always come back here during the holidays. We'll sneak out to meet you. The fact that you are moving away will not impact our friendship even scarcely. But you MUST go. You must go and live a life you were born to live; one that you truly deserve," I tried to console him. But no amount of consoling could have prevented the outpour that followed, the tears, the agony reflected on each drop of tear; the hopelessness and affliction that had then blighted his face is beyond the capacity of words to describe. Somewhere in our hearts, we knew that our words of solace and assurance were going to fail in front of his tears. So, we did the next best thing – besides trying to allay his fears – we hugged him; all five of us. We hugged him to let him know that he was not alone; that even though he had all the reasons to be dismal and crestfallen, we would not leave him alone in his despondency; that his melancholy was not his alone, but of all of us. To this day, when I reminisce about my village days, I always think of that embrace as a symbol of the truest and purest friendship that could have graced the earth.

17

FAREWELLS AND GOODBYES

Vihaan did, eventually, leave for the city the subsequent week with Rihan Bhaiya and Durga Di, although with much hesitation and entreaties. We met every day during that week, we met Dadu, and we went to school. Vihaan also met Dr Adam and thanked him once again for treating him and his concussion. When the day arrived for their departure, the five of us, accompanied by Dadu and Ma gathered around their house to bid them adieu. It was a strange day. The sun seemed to have forgotten its sheen in the clouds, and the clouds were scattered in feathery spots all over the sky. They were so thin and seemed so emaciated, that a spectre could have easily passed through them, and still remain visible to the eye. There was a soft, light breeze, which I thought had been sent by the clouds to dry our faces.

I had expected Vihaan to cry for one last time upon seeing us, but he didn't. He was as sombre as the morning that was to witness this gut-wrenching farewell. His face was pale and eyes dry, though red. There was not a line of frown on his forehead, but his mouth was cemented in a resolute, but painful submission and commitment. He had on his face not even the slightest dash of any turmoil that might have been besetting him internally. I was in awe of him at that moment. I have earlier mentioned small children who feared life. Now, while alluding to it, I will once again talk about small children who look upon life, or are rather compelled to look upon life, as a challenge, as something meant to be endured, and not lived. The poise and stoicism with which Vihaan had accepted this challenge were incredulous. I could not restrain my tears when I saw Durga Di and Vihaan board their luggage – I was being separated from my sister and a friend who was no less than a brother. But when I glanced at Vihaan and saw his passive face, I decided to compose myself. I was parting from only two of my pillars. He had to part from five. My pain itself felt to me unutterably excruciating. His was unfathomable to me.

I am, once again, at a loss to describe Durga Di's countenance since her face, as on her wedding day, was veiled. I did see a tiny drop of tear fall on her clutched fist, but it was immediately wiped off. It would not have been approved by her in-laws that a married woman should cry on parting with her sister or her maternal family. Separation was a sacrifice meant to be undertaken with the utmost pride – expressing distress in such situations was looked down upon and still is. Durga Di had a tremendous understanding of these conventions, and could thus, easily abide by them whenever necessary.

We said our goodbyes, renewed our promises and made some fresh ones. Confessions, or rather reiterations, of love and affection were pronounced and reciprocated. Blessings were given; prayers were offered; and a few solitary, discreet tears were shed. At the end of this all, after about fifteen minutes, Rihan Bhaiya, Durga Di and Vihaan embarked on the taxi that had been hired for their departure and journey. We stayed there for a couple of minutes more, waving at the taxi which drew farther and farther away with each wave, and closer to the new life which awaited them in a strange, alien place. And just like that, our sun left its sky.

When we were certain that their car could no more be seen, we withdrew and went our separate ways – Vihaan's parents went inside their empty house, Ma proceeded to prepare the afternoon meal, Dadu proceeded towards his shop and the remaining five of us, obviously, headed towards our retreat, the mango tree.

Vihaan's father made a vain attempt at trying to stop us, particularly me, but Dadu checked him. I saw Dadu put his hand on his shoulder and give me a stern but compassionate and indulgent look. He had no choice but to yield.

The departure of these pivotal members of our lives, expedited life in the villages as though it had been lifted and thrust on a mountain slope covered in an icy sheet. The subsequent week was so monotonous, it would have made monotony bow its head down in shame. But I have always believed that unnatural placidity is a foreboding of impending disaster; or something at least close to it. The next week commenced as naturally as any other – I woke up in the morning, escaped from the window, washed my face in the well, went to the mango tree, and waited for others to join me. This was the plan initially. But when I reached the mango tree, I heard a whisper call out my name from somewhere. It was a hurried whisper and the urgency in it could be identified very distinctly.

"Tamanna! Look up!" And I saw Eva and Eric perched on one of the branches.

"What are you doing up there?" I yelled, looking up with scrunched eyes. The sun was very strong that day.

"*Shh*! Keep your voice down! Climb up!" said Eva.

"But why?" I can be stubborn at times.

"And you say I'm annoying," Eric remarked to Eva.

"Tamanna, just climb up! We'll tell you what happened," Eva urged. I obeyed this time and was sitting on another branch like theirs in no time. When your house doesn't satisfy you, you tend to seek excitement and thrill outside; and believe me when I say, climbing a tree, especially when it's a competition between you and your friends is one of the most thrilling activities a child can enjoy.

"Now! Why are we sitting here?" I asked as soon as I was comfortably ensconced.

Just then, we heard another voice. "Where is everybody? Aren't we usually the last ones to reach here?" It was Taheera.

"We're here!" Eric said in a loud whisper.

"What are you doing up there? And why are you whispering?" enquired Nazia.

"Did you catch a cold? Did you lose your voice? But you were fine yesterday!" exclaimed Taheera. As I mentioned earlier, she was younger than us by a couple of more years. This predisposed her to sudden, extreme outbursts.

"My voice is alright, Taheera!" Eric replied in his normal voice, exasperated.

"*Shh*! Eric, shut up! Nazia, Taheera, climb up, and we'll tell you." It was Eva again.

Once they were comfortably seated in another one of the thick, strong branches, Eva commenced her story.

"Something is going to happen today, something bad."

"What thing? And bad?"

"Eric and I heard some men talking. Their tones were hushed, so we had to strain our ears. And we had to be careful about not letting those men spot us, so we hid behind another house and eavesdropped."

"What were they talking about?"

"Apparently, a woman, presumably from our village, has been raped and is currently confined inside her house. She was found unconscious and bleeding behind some bushes in one of your villages; the men didn't mention which. She had gone to visit a friend along with her four-year-old son. The son is nowhere to be found. So, it's most likely that he has been kidnapped."

"That's terrible!" I cried.

"When did this happen? Did they look for the boy properly?" asked Nazia.

"It must have happened a couple of days back. I don't know how much or how long they searched for the boy. But what we do know is that those men believe that the rape and the kidnapping were undertaken by someone from either of your villages," she said looking at me and Nazia, worried, her eyes implying the ruinous repercussions such an empty and thoughtless belief is usually capable of engendering. Her mind was intuitively aware of what was soon to become another scarring experience.

"But it could have been anyone! What if somebody from your village did it and then carried the woman to either of our villages and left her there?" I asked.

"We thought so too," Eric replied gravely.

"The villagers are not going to consider that a possibility. It's like taking an infected, dead lamb and meticulously placing it inside the lion's den. The brutes will devour it anyway," explained Nazia.

"Precisely. Further, not only will it be suicidal for the brutes, but in the process of satisfying their hunger, they will ruin the entire jungle," added Eva.

"What are you saying? Lion, lamb, *brooot*…we were talking about those men! When did we reach to animals?" Taheera asked, tears welling up in her eyes. She could sense the tension in our voices, but she was still too young to comprehend the analogies.

"What they mean is, there is a chance, I don't know how big or small, that there might be another riot… another *danga*," answered Eric, nervously.

"What is that?" Taheera asked innocently. She reminded me of my first time witnessing a riot. I had been slightly younger than her when I had made my acquaintance with this terrifying phenomenon. That was also the moment when I had familiarised myself with what emotions a hatred towards something entails. Despite being born and living in an abusive household, and living with an obnoxious father and equally repugnant pair of grandparents, I had managed to prevent any strong, violent emotion from corroding my heart. But this was not to be for long. It still pains me to think that a mere four-year-old was coerced into feeling *hate*, even before she had gained consciousness of an emotion called "love." To think that it was now Taheera's turn to go through what I had endured five years back, ached me; even now, it does.

"You'll know it when you see it," Nazia replied.

"Is that a fire there?"

"It has begun."

"Should we hide somewhere?"

"Let's climb higher up. This tree is sufficiently thick to hide all of us."

None of us could see clearly what ensued thus. The sun was scorching hot, the air humid, the clouds absconding. Once again, any sort of relief, be it clouds in the sky, wind in the air, or conscience of the mind, had been totally abandoned. The foliage was too dense to be penetrated. But it did not hinder us from peeking through the small spaces, left by the leaves for our leisure – or torment. Eric broke a thin, long twig from the branch he was sitting on and pushed aside a small, but thick cluster of leaves on his left for us to gaze at the spectacle. After a while, we could distinguish all kinds of people – men, women, children of all ages, old, young. Nazia and Taheera were sitting on the branch just below mine, and I saw Nazia pull her sister closer to her. The little girl responded by burying her head in her sister's protective shoulder. The two sisters shared an incredible bond and were immensely fond of each other. Nazia often amused herself by teasing her sister, but whenever the situation required, she did not hesitate before standing as a shield between her and the ruthless assaults of the barbarians disguised in their family. She was a passionate girl by nature, but because of having led a restrained, caged life, she never found an activity or a hobby which could potentially sustain her energy. It was only when Taheera came along that she finally found the locus of all the fervour and love awaiting liberation from her closed, but impassioned heart. Her commitment towards her sister probably also arose from her determination to not let her be subjected to the atrocities that she had to endure during the years when Taheera was still a fantasy, and even after that.

Taheera, likewise, loved her sister very dearly. She saw in Nazia a guardian angel, who would – and could – never defer from safeguarding her against life's unforeseen threats. Having failed in finding a pillar in her older family members, she found solace in her sister and directed all her devotion and confidence to the one person whom she believed, and trusted, to be her own. She was an affectionate girl, which made it impossible to not be charmed by her little idiosyncrasies. Since she was the youngest of us all, it did not take us long to assume the responsibility for her security at all times.

People were running everywhere. Who went which way was impossible to decipher. Houses in all three villages were being torched without paying the slightest heed to whom it may have housed. A reckless savagery had suddenly gained the foreground. It would be wrong to assume that the spectacle we were witnessing, open-mouthed and wide-eyed, was thoughtless; that it was propagated by unthinking individuals. People *were* thinking – they must have been – about their old parents, young children, spouses, livelihood, farms, livestock; a safe refuge or a shelter, a hiding place; whether those were their last moments, or will they be fortunate enough to survive another one of these ghastly riots; what had they ever done to deserve such mercy? But one thing I was sure of was that there could have been only but one, singular thought in the minds of the orchestrators – complete destruction; annihilation; not to spare even an iota of forbearance on whomever they laid eyes on. The fire that was blazing in people's hearts did not fail to evade us. Within only a few minutes, frenzied cries of all hues had filled the air – children shouting for their mothers and fathers; men yelling at their wives and old parents; infants wailing, unknowing that this might be their last cry. The event of 1 December 1983 was repeated in front of me. The last time, I had averted my eyes, but this time, I kept them fixed, unwavering. And yet, I cannot describe that morning in too many details; either my mind does not allow me to conjure it, or it has completely erased them from plausible cognizance. I don't know which. I heard Taheera's stifled sobs and saw Nazia clutch her tighter. They reminded me of when Durga Di had salvaged me from our burning village about six years back.

We sat there on that tree, perched on those branches, the whole of that morning. Nazia had tempted Taheera into sleep by softly humming her a lullaby. The four nine-year-olds now remained the sole witnesses of what had transpired in the course of that treacherous morning. Not a word had been uttered by any of us. Our throats were dry and our faces wet. Hunger gnawed at the deepest pits of our stomachs. Our bodies were stiff. We did not realise this till everything had subsided and dense smoke, instead of frantic cries, now veiled the air. We had hid there in that mango tree in trepidation of being seen till dusk. We decided to disembark at this moment. Eric and I went down first to confirm that we were alone and that there was no danger lurking in the bushes. We then gestured for Eva and Nazia to climb down. Nazia hung the half-asleep Taheera on her shoulders, and with Eva's help, the three came down. Our eyes took some time to adjust to the sooty air. The crackling sound of the fires dulled the painful moans and wails of the people who had fallen victim to the brutish minds of the rioters.

"What are we going to do now?" Eric ventured to ask.

"Let's go and see if Dadu is okay. Maybe we'll find Mahira Ma'am and Ashwat Sir there too," Eva suggested. This suggestion might seem startling due to its lack of any familial concern. But is it truly startling? Whom did we have to be concerned about?

We commenced our expedition from the mango tree to Dadu's shop and took our same old path between the tall wheat stalks of my village and Eva and Eric's. This path was neither plain nor were the wheat stalks tall, anymore. There were tiny specks of blood hither and thither on the ground and on the stalks; the stalks slashed in some parts, and some uprooted, destroying even the slightest prospect of a farmer redeeming his old economy. We knew that our secret passage had been trespassed and was no safer than wandering in full view, unconcealed. But we still ventured ahead, trying to not ponder over the possibility of a man, or a group of men, lurching at us from nowhere.

An unnatural amount of time seemed to have passed by the time we reached Dadu's shop. As expected, we found Mahira Ma'am and Ashwat Sir sitting inside the shop with Dadu, drinking tea.

"Hello!" I exclaimed, glad that they were all okay. But my good-natured exclamation startled them out of their wits.

It was only when we had advanced a bit closer that we could get a better look at them. Mahira Ma'am's hands were quivering, which probably induced her into clasping her teacup with both hands to keep it a tad steady. Her hair was badly dishevelled, and she was sweating profusely, but her face betrayed no sign of any internal angst. Even though she wasn't in her usual amicable temper, she still was quite tranquil; or at least seemed to be, because genuine composure does not easily rattle. Ashwat Sir was sitting on a stool and looked grave. He had a deep frown on his forehead. His mouth was fixed in a pensive rigidity and his eyes bore an expression of intense rage. His hands were relatively steadier but clutched the teacup so tightly that one could easily trace his veins. A tiny drop of red, flowing down his forehead and down his cheek, dropped on his arm, causing me to glance at his head. His black, thick hair was entirely wet, except for one blotch which seemed darker than usual. Contradictorily, Dadu truly seemed much calmer and more in sync with his wits, even though he was staring blankly ahead in front of him, pondering over something. He was sitting on his chair completely laid back and coolly sipping his tea when we broke his reverie.

"OH, GOD! Tamanna! You should at least warn!" cried Mahira Ma'am.

"Why? Who else did you think would greet you?" asked Eric.

"Look at the school," pointed Ashwat Sir.

It was burnt completely and absolutely. Every inch of it was blackened. Not a spot remained which could boast of its earlier glory. Its extreme left end was destroyed from the roof, giving it a teetering appearance, with the right end lying on the ground and nothing remaining of its lower portion, while the roof of this end was still intact. Fragmented pieces of our wooden chairs and tables lay on the rubble, scattered. The storeroom, which had sheltered Nazia and Taheera was lost in the debris too. There was water sprouting out of a couple of pipes in the areas which previously served as the bathrooms. On venturing a little ahead, we found some of the library books too, lying – torn and burnt – on the ruin. Tiny, shattered pieces of glass, some dusty, others bloody, adorned the wreck. The bushes surrounding the building too were scorched.

I raised my head and took a step back to get a full view of the site. I once again scoured over the scenery in its entirety, as much as my mind would allow my eyes to move, and suddenly felt the image blurring. No; I didn't faint. With a heaving chest and quivering mouth, I broke down crying. I fell to my knees on the ground and cried. I cried as if I had seen the end of my world. Containing everything within me now felt intractable. I was merely a nine-year-old after all, and these successive losses were too cumbersome to sustain, too overwhelming to weather. There is only a limit to which the heart can sustain heavy blows, and the vision of the school crossed that limit by far. Eva knelt down beside me and joined me in my lamentation. Taheera was awoken by now, and seeing the two of us cry, she too loosened her heart's chains.

Our guardians soon joined us, and we wept together, mourning the sight of our almost-dead dream.

"Tamanna! Where have you been the whole day? Do you know how scared we were?" Ma cried. We decided to return to our respective houses to see how good or bad the conditions were. They were mostly good.

"Scared? For me?"

"Yes, you fool!"

"Are you lying to me, or to yourself, Ma? I don't believe that anybody in this house was scared for me except you."

"You believe what you want."

"Do you even care that your grandfather is dead?" bellowed Rahul Bhaiya. This piece of information did not stir in me even the slightest pity or grief. For me, my grandfather was no more than another actor in my life who made living miserable.

"He's dead?" I asked plainly.

"Yes."

"Oh."

"Oh? Is that all you have to say for your dead grandfather?"

"What else do you want me to say?"

"You imbecile!"

"That's enough!" Ma intervened. "Rahul, go to your grandmother and see if she needs anything. Naveen, go to your father. See if he needs any help."

"And what will Tamanna do?" asked Naveen.

"Why do you need to know that? Do what you have been asked to," Ma replied curtly.

Once we were alone, Ma took me to the kitchen, sat me down, and said, "Tamanna, I don't know where you were this entire morning. But I'm glad that you are safe and untouched. And I hope your friends are fine too?"

"Yes. We were together."

"Okay. Good. Now, I will have to ask of you a favour."

"What?"

"To act."

"Act?"

"Yes. Act that you are sad at your grandfather's demise." I stared at her, unbelieving. "I know that his death does not sadden you; nor does it sadden me. He was a spineless bootlicker who only enabled your father to become the man he is today. I know that even you believe that. But we are women living in a society where people would rather attend to an injured snake, than render their attention or compassion, or any of those nicer things, to a woman. We have to make compromises. Sometimes, it's the compromise of your life, sometimes character, sometimes self-respect, and sometimes principles. I know that you are assertive, and unafraid to say what you think or show how you feel. But right now, I'm begging you to forgo these qualities. They will take you a long way once you are out of this hell. But you need to stay alive to get out! And if your father sees you remorseless, I'm afraid he will not allow another breath to enter your body. Naveen must have already told your father about our discussion here. That damage is done. But we can prevent any further damage if you comply with me." I saw the desperate earnestness glistening once again in Ma's eyes (previously, I had seen it when she had threatened Durga Di into the marriage). But she knew that threats would fall in vain in front of me. She had to resort to logic.

"Okay."

"Okay?"

"Okay." I nodded my head.

"Thank you," Ma replied, relieved.

What commenced thus need not be elaborated in dialogues. It began with the usual – my father came, hollering my name. Naveen had, in fact, snitched about me. But I did not respond to his thrashing and cursing as I normally would have. I protested on a tangent. I led him to believe that my reaction was not a result of inadequacy of emotions, but rather a manifestation of grave shock; that it had all been a misunderstanding; that I was not as insensitive and loveless as my brothers perceived me to be; and that even though my grandfather and I were never on the greatest of terms, he was still family. This protestation calmed my father down, and I also detected a hint of the likeness of some repentance for having yelled at me for no reason on the day of his father's demise. He turned to Naveen and told him not to be so quick to judge, and with that, he left to arrange for the funeral.

"You are such a sly little brat," Rahul Bhaiya whispered through clenched teeth, contemptuously.

"Rahul, mind your language," Ma replied, sternly.

"I will, once she starts minding her behaviour."

"You have no reason to be bothered by her behaviour. She is not your daughter. But you are my son and your behaviour and contempt towards your own blood is definitely bothering me right now." Ma had easily closed any opportunity for me to retort.

"And I'm grateful that she's not my daughter because I will not rear mine the way you have reared yours. And you've suddenly found your voice, haven't you? – with grandfather dead, grandmother in mourning and Papa busy in arrangements?"

"Get out of my sight right now!" Ma pronounced emphatically each syllable of that sentence, and with as much ire and vehemence as her frail body could muster. At that moment, she probably saw a reflection of her husband on her eldest son; and what is worse for a mother than to see her own son become the man she most detested; to endow another woman with a husband she would never want for herself or her daughters – that is, if given the choice. I was rather taken aback by this confrontation. In nine years of my life, I had always seen her as subservient and timid. Her hidden valour came as a pleasant surprise.

My father returned about an hour and a half later, drenched in blood and sweat, panting.

"What happened to you? Are you injured?" Ma cried in incredulity.

"No. Get me a glass of water," was his answer. Ma darted off to get him water, and instructed me to fetch a dry towel, while he flung himself on a chair, exhausted.

"Did you check in on Vihaan's parents?" I dared to ask once he had finished his drink and dried his face with the towel. He glared at me for a few seconds before answering, "Yes, I did."

"Are they okay?" I asked, not caring for the steel glass on the stool beside him which could be hurled at me any time.

"No. Somebody hit his father on the head with a liquor bottle, and then lighted his hair on fire." This information received strong exclamations from everyone in the room; me too. But make no mistake; I gasped not out of sympathy for the man, but out of sheer abhorrence at the effecting of such a vicious and despicable act. What hatred or slandering of the soul could have led someone to these measures was incomprehensible and unimaginable to me. The fact that someone could even be in possession of such a rotten mind saddened me more than what that mind had occasioned.

"Was he taken to the hospital?" enquired Rahul Bhaiya.

"I took him."

"Did Dr Adam see him? What did he say?" Ma further probed.

"Yes, he was there. He told me that he will do his best. But I could see on his face that he too was not very hopeful."

"What does he fear?" I asked.

"That even if he lives, his brain will not be the same."

And it wasn't. They had to shave his head to operate on his brain. He could never again regrow his hair, and the scars, which the glass pieces had imprinted on his head, were as clear as black oil cutting through the clear water of a lake. The part of his skull which had to be cut open for the operation, and was sewed back on, could easily be detected because of its symmetry; the scars of the glass pieces were rather generously strewn all over his head. Mentally, he was reduced to a baby who had not yet been toilet trained, spoke illegibly, was unaware of where his hands and legs flew or hit, was susceptible to hysterics and had absolutely no powers of any mental cognition. It was a deplorable state but beyond remedy. "It's a miracle he is alive," Dr Adam had remarked upon completion of the surgery. Vihaan's mother had to forgo the onus of a wife and adopt the duty of a nurse-cum-maid. Rihan Bhaiya often implored them to live with him in the city, where they could take better care of the disabled father, but his mother consistently declined the offer, her reasoning being that she wanted to breathe her last breath at a place which had been hers since she had first felt its air, and had his father not lost his mind to the riot, he too would have felt the same. Rihan Bhaiya had no other option but to succumb to her arguments, so he began sending home double the amount of money that he previously used to. This did not create many financial upheavals back in his city home, accredited to Durga Di's newfound job.

Eva and Eric's father owned an ancestral shop. This shop would provide sustenance when farming betrayed them. It was either managed by a cousin who lived nearby or sometimes by their mother. It had been in their family for the last three generations and had been passed on from one generation to the next unchanged, though at times, tainted. It had seen the ravages of time and society but perished in this riot. It had been set on fire, and very meticulously at that. Whoever had done the deed, had first poured glycerine all over the place, thrown in some dry wood, glued the doors using an adhesive, and tossed in a lit torch through a window, and then sealed that too. Yes, the task did require a lot of consideration, strategy and patience to be carried out in a dangerously capricious surrounding, and the person has my highest admiration in enabling a successful undertaking, but also my greatest loathe and disdain for channelling such a superior mind into destroying a family legacy, that was accountable for most, if not the entirety, of the family's income.

Nazia and Taheera, after deliberating with us for a long time, went back to their house, this time, escorted by Ashwat Sir. They had not seen their father or their grandparents since the day we had liberated them from that prison. This was a huge risk that had to be taken, but more so out of pragmatic concerns – only to check whether they were all dead or still alive.

On reaching their destination, they saw their house in a mess – the windows broken, the door ajar and hanging loosely by a couple of rusted hinges, patches of red on the walls, a part of the house blackened, as though it had been intended to be set on fire but was prematurely extinguished. It was silent and ostensibly empty.

"Hello?"

"Where is everybody?"

"Must have fled."

"Then who put out the fire?"

"Let's go inside the rooms and see."

Their search did not take much time. The first room that they entered granted them their award. Their grandfather lay motionless on the floor, an entire pool of blood beside and above his head. Ashwat Sir checked his pulse and tried to determine his breathing. He was dead.

Their grandmother lay beside her husband. She had not sustained any apparent injury, but she too was dead – probably out of shock or a cardiac arrest.

Their father remained alive, though severely injured. With the help of the neighbours, they took all three of them to the hospital – two of them were brought dead and the third, critical. His right arm had to be amputated. The left arm had sustained a few fractures, which, as fate would have it, did not get much time to heal. Both his legs had to be operated upon three and four times respectively for both had endured extremely deep cuts, like those from either a butcher's knife or a sickle, rendering him paralysed for the remainder of his life. With all his weapons (except his tongue) unavailing, he was obligated to be tied to his bed – he could not eat on his own, drink on his own, go to the bathroom on his own, bathe on his own, or for that matter, beat his own. This vicissitude, of having lost both the parents *and* his agility on one fateful day, somehow subdued him. Nazia and Taheera were employed in his service, but he had abandoned all his curses, antipathy, and his infamous temper. He would lie on his bed the whole day, barely opening his mouth or moving himself, except when absolutely required. One tragic day had done to the man what even God and Satan combined could not have achieved.

Not to forget, the two sisters were restored their house, and could finally partake of the sweet, but peculiar taste of a peaceful life. But this was not to last long.

18

A REUNION

Three months, two weeks and four days later, we decided to sneak out of the village and into the city to meet Vihaan. It was a Saturday, so we knew that he'd have no school. We – the five of us as one, and Vihaan – had exchanged a few letters in this period, describing chiefly, how all of us were coping in our disrupted and altered environments. The letters sent to Vihaan were always written by me while being dictated by everyone, one after the other, since I had the best handwriting. After a point, the content of our letters would grow mundane and repetitive, but not our spirits, until one fine morning, when we decided to reply to his last letter in person. We had his address. We just needed some money, which we stole from our respective households. (I did not steal. I simply asked my mother to return the favour she had asked of me three months back, and the money was granted, although a bit reluctantly. Her issue was not with respect to the money, but to the fact that a bunch of nine-year-olds wanted to journey to the city alone. So, I lied to her and assured her that Ashwat Sir would be accompanying us. Little did I know that this was to be my last conversation with her.)

We decided to take the route used by vehicles to transport people and goods between the villages and the city. Crossing the river would have required a boat and would have definitely roused Dadu's attention. Had he known about our scheme, he would not have allowed us to venture into the city alone. So, we agreed to hire a taxi from the nearest taxi stand after entering the city, which would eventually take us to our destination.

We embarked upon our mission at five in the morning, when everyone in our houses was fast asleep, since we had resolved upon returning the very same day. It was a particularly windy day – the trees were dancing along to the breeze, sheltering the tiny sparrows and goldfinches who were too delicate to withstand the wind. The air was misty, and a fleet of black clouds were steadily approaching us from the north. The white and orange *shiuli* flowers, which had abundantly festooned the bushes of our villages in the past two to three weeks, lay strewn across our path, their spotless petals grubby with dirt. An eerie silence had enveloped the villages. Most people were still engulfed in their slumber, save those who were incapable of finding some repose even in their dreams. Even the presence of these hermits did not disturb the silence looming over the villages – such was the profundity of that thick blanket, and such was the lassitude of those stray souls.

The road to the city was not via any of the three villages. It was a separate road, with scattered potholes, ditches and pits, and lay in the direction opposite Dadu's shop, leading from the mango tree. The clouds had forewarned us of the impending downpour, so all of us carried our umbrellas with us, along with a couple of scarves each to conceal ourselves.

By the time we reached a taxi stand and could witness the early hustle of city life, it was about 6:30 a.m.

"Hello, Sir! Will you take us to –Road, please?" Eva asked the first idle taxi driver. He had a half-smoked cigarette between his index and middle finger and was leaning sulkily against his car. He was averagely tall and would not have been above thirty-five, going by his physiognomy. But his face said otherwise. There were dark shadows beneath his black, enervated eyes, forming two deep gorges on his tired, brown face. So controlled were his eyes that the sudden appearance of a bunch of children could not elicit the slightest flicker of change in their expression.

He scrutinized us from top to bottom, and from one member to the other, with that same torpidity before answering, "Why not… Do you have money?"

"Yes. How much will you charge?"

"Do you want me to give you some discount?"

"Why?"

"Because you're children," he replied with a raised eyebrow.

"Is that allowed?" Eric asked, astonished.

"Not really. But how will the authorities know unless you report me to them?"

"We don't intend to do any such thing," assured Nazia.

"Good."

"But if we don't pay in full, what about the remainder of the expense? Who will give that?" enquired Taheera.

"You need not bother yourself with that. Come on now. Hop in!" he commanded with as much impassivity as his eyes bore their unchanging enervation.

And we hopped in. Eva, Nazia, Taheera and I sat behind, and Eric seated himself on the passenger's seat.

This was our first time riding a car. It had a stereo attached to it, but it had a hole in it (an external volume control probably went there). The face of the stereo had several scratches on it, rendering it barely possible to see the channel number, the time, or whatever other information it was meant to display. The seat covers too were torn from more than a few places. Once we had closed the doors, the air inside the car suddenly felt too sultry and fetid to be suffered without lowering the windows. Moreover, even though we had read about the air pollution levels in cities, the weather was unusually pleasant that day, and as I pulled down my side of the window, a gentle breeze caressed my red, flushed face, exhausted from the day's excursion, and I closed my eyes, leaned my head against the side window and unknowingly, a faint and tranquil smile alighted my lips; clearing my brows, I let my stiff shoulders fall down to a peaceful resignation.

"What's your name?" Eric asked our driver after a quarter of an hour.

"Rahman."

"I'm Eric." This piece of information was acknowledged by a simple nodding of the head.

"Does this work?" Eric asked Rahman Uncle, pointing at the stereo.

"Why not!" He took out a volume control from a pocket beside his seat and handed it to Eric.

"Put it on that hole. Press it slightly, and then turn it clockwise," he instructed Eric.

Eric did so, and a faint sound of a song playing on the radio emerged.

"Jeene ke liye socha hi nahi
Dard sambhalane honge,
Muskurayein to muskurane ke
Karz utaarne honge,
Ho muskuraun kabhi to lagta hai
Jaise hothon pe karz rakha hai"
[Never thought that to live
Is to bear the burden of pains,
That to smile is to
Incur the debt of that smile.
When I smile and if I smile,
My lips carry the debt of my smile.]
And I dozed off listening to these words and softly humming to its music.

"Tamanna. Tamanna. Wake up. We're here," were the words I heard next.

"Let's throw a bottle of water on her! Only then will the sleepy head wake up!"

"Shut up, Eric."

"Oh, come on! I'm so excited to see Vihaan after so long! How can she still be sleeping? Her excitement should be double that of mine! She'll be meeting her sister too!"

"She must be very tired. Wake up, Tamanna!"

I opened my eyes unsteadily at this last piece of enjoinment. I *was* tired. I hadn't had a sound sleep in the last week, for reasons unknown to me. I had recurring dreams each night. But they weren't repetitive in their content, only a strange consciousness of everything being red. I was the focal point of all those dreams; a passive spectator to a frenzied commotion that surrounded me the second I submitted myself to exhaustion. But when I woke up, I'd never remember any detail about the commotion – what led to it, who was involved, why nobody could see me, whether there were familiar faces, whether I thought about escaping, etc. The only aspect that dominated my recollection of the previous night was RED.

"Where are we? Have we reached?" I asked rubbing my eyes drowsily.

"Yes, sleeping beauty! We've reached! Come on, now! Show some enthusiasm!" Eric exclaimed.

"We've reached? Then why are we still sitting here? Let's go!" I was fully awake now.

"And who is going to pay me? The President of The United States?" asked Rahman Uncle.

"Oh! I'm sorry! How much do you need?" Eva asked.

"I *need* much more than you will ever be able to give me, child. But right now, this ride cost you a hundred rupees. So, just give me half of it." She handed him the required amount, and proceeded to ask, "Do you have a piece of paper and a pencil? Or a pen?"

"Yes. Why?"

"Can I have them for a minute, please?" He rummaged inside the pocket once again and gave her a pen and a torn, dirty piece of paper. Eva went behind the car and noted down its number once we had deboarded our taxi. She came to the front and knocked on our driver's windowpane. He lowered it down without a shadow of perplexity on his face.

"Here's your pen. We might not have enough money right now, but I promise you, I will return the remaining half one day: when I earn my own money. Pinky promise."

He stared at Eva for a few seconds before replying, "I will wait for that day," and took his pen back. His expression changed in those few seconds. His lips curled up in what seemed like a smile unaccustomed to its function. I saw a twinkle in his eyes too when his lips formed that subtle, imperceptible smile. There was a certain pride in his smile. No, it was not vanity. But a reassurance, like a consolation to a beaten, dejected mind – one that has lost all hopes to ever be able to witness any goodness hidden in the world and one which no more engages in the futile attempts of searching for that goodness; one which already believes that there *is* no goodness left in the world. But Eva's little gesture felt like a fresh beam of hope meant to dispel that gloom in his eyelids which had eclipsed any potential sunshine. There is no one word which can describe that expression. If there is, then I'm not aware of it. But one word that does come to my mind when I visualise his face, and probably comes nearest to doing justice to that emotion, is *ethereal.*

We left after thanking him for the ride. He had dropped us beside a cluster of similar-looking, but asymmetrical buildings. There were about five to six such clusters before and after us on that road. Each building held absolutely no resemblance with the one preceding it. All of them were dissimilar in breadth and height; they were coloured differently (some only seemed different because they had discoloured), chiefly in different shades of brown, blue and pink; some had posters and advertisements stuck on them (of celebrities or local actors and musicians), while some were bare; some were relatively well-maintained than their counterparts, while the same counterparts could barely allow their houses to be habitable.

These differences were apparent even in the same building. Some floors were decorated with plants and ebullient, fresh flowers, while some had the paint crust hanging from the walls. Some seemed almost spotlessly clean, as much as the neighbourhood could allow and the eyes could deem worthy, while some others had mud patches of balls or tiny hands imprinted on them. Some went as far as arranging a sitting area in their balconies with a table and two small chairs, while some contained a wooden ladder or a box of paint, with the paint dripping on the floor.

It was a sight with too many contradictions, but irrespective of that, or the unpleasantry of the conditions of some houses, we were still awed. The view we held in front of ourselves was new to us, not to our imaginations, but to our reality. We had read about buildings and city life and imagined how different they would be from the circumstances we lived in. We had imagined the various skylines, we had imagined a flight of birds adorning the sky above those buildings, we had imagined children flying kites or dancing in the rain on their rooftops, we had imagined aeroplanes soaring higher and faster than the puffs of cotton hanging from the heavens leaving behind a trail of vapour in the azure sky, but we had never imagined how we would place ourselves amongst these whimsical amusements. A group of children inured only to mud, thatch and straw, if and when placed in front of bricks, cement and paint, will naturally want to absorb all that their tiny minds can accommodate.

"What was the house number, Tamanna?" Eva's voice broke my trance.

"F-032. 'F' must be the building."

"What's '032'?"

"There should be one digit indicating the floor, and another indicating the apartment number because there is more than one apartment on each floor. See?" said Nazia, pointing towards the said building.

"So, 0, 3 and 2. Which digit is for which?" asked Eric, perplexed.

"Let's ask someone," suggested Eva. There was a vegetable vendor just beside our building, spraying water on his vegetables and waving a cloth over them. We went to him and asked. "Hello! We are new to this place and need your help in finding this house," Eva said, thrusting the address paper in front of his face. The man examined us with a pair of seemingly hyper-vigilant and distrustful eyes before he replied, in a rather sour voice, "Why would you trust me?"

"We don't have any other option," Eva answered looking him straight in the eyes. He rested his gaze on her for a while, and probably upon finding something of substance in her eyes, he complied, "That girl was right," indicating Nazia. "The '3' is the floor. '2' is the house number."

"Thank you so much!" The five of us exclaimed in unison, and we scampered off.

The building that we entered was not very well maintained from within. The walls had *gutka* (tobacco) spits on the edges – some dry and very faded red, and others relatively wetter. There were thick cobwebs in a few corners with flies or tiny caterpillars stuck on them. The walls themselves were of a dirty cream colour. I ran a cursory finger on them and collected a thin layer of dust on my fingertip. The stairs too could not boast of wellness. I found a couple of them wider than the rest, with occasional dents on their edges. They were plain and concrete and went up in a spiral. The railings meant for our support, could not be touched without allowing tiny chips of the reddish-brown rust, formed on top of the iron, to stick to our palms. There were tiny cobwebs in the railings too. '*Either there are too many spiders here, or just a few large families of spiders,*' I remember thinking, glancing at the sheer number of cobwebs.

We finally reached the third floor and pressed a switch beside the door of house no. 2. There were two houses on each floor, and each house that we passed, would have repelled me if I were to venture inside them, even if I had been brought up in dirt and squirt. But the one outside of which we had stopped, was unceremoniously impeccable – "unceremonious" because it ruthlessly brought shame upon the other apartments, and made them look nothing better than a cottage in a squalor; more so, because it unabashedly stood taller and grander than its mates. The door was of iron and had been painted with a fresh coat of brown paint. A "welcome" sign hung from the top, the thread supporting the sign taped neatly to the corners of the door's frame. Another thread, taped at the ends, hung across the breadth of the topmost edge of the door, from which, were dangling four strings of fresh, unwilted flowers – two of them were entirely of yellow marigold, and the other two were of dark red marigold. A few inches above the frame of the door, there was a plate with the house number "F-032" inscribed on it in bold. Beside the door on the right, and some space above the switch, was another plate, containing their surname "-s'" in beautiful cursive. Both the plates had a rustic texture, and the engravings had a jet-black hue, with specks of white whenever and wherever light fell on them.

Vihaan opened the door upon hearing the bell. Imagine a colour palette. Wet its surface with some clear water. Then, drop a few beads of white, grey and black on it, and then mix all of them, but not so much that they lose their parent shade. Now, take any other colour – Persian blue, yellow, maroon, lime green, or tangerine – and drop a thick pinch of it on your mixture, and then watch that one colour gradually seep through the grey and dominate the palette. That is what happened on his face.

"What on earth are you doing here? How did you even reach here? Whose help did you ask for? Does anybody know that you're here? Did anyone else come with you? Or did you come on your own? But how could you come on your own?"

"We'll answer all your questions. Let's first sit down here, right outside your house, since you don't seem to invite us in," Eric replied, sarcastically.

"No, no! I'm sorry, I forgot. Come in, come in!"

He invited us into a small but cosy living room on the right of the main entrance. It had two sofa sets of a faded lilac and a plain yet comely centre table. Facing the living room was the dining area, adjoining which, was the kitchen. Between the kitchen and the living room, went a long corridor, at the end of which were two rooms. Their house wasn't particularly ornamented, but it carried the warmth and comfort of a peaceful living and a loving family.

"Come, sit here," he pointed towards the sofa set. "I'll get water. You must be hungry! I'll get some biscuits too." And he sprinted to the kitchen.

"Now. Answer my questions. How did you come here?"

"In the taxi."

"Where did you get it?"

"At the taxi stand, outside our village."

"Who accompanied you till there?"

"No one."

"Why not?"

"No one knows that we're here."

"No one?"

"Not a soul."

"Why not?"

"Do you think anyone would have allowed us if we had asked them?"

"What about Dadu, or Ashwat Sir, or Mahira Ma'am?"

"Dadu keeps his shop open even on weekends nowadays, so we couldn't disturb him. Ashwat Sir and Mahira Ma'am have been busy rebuilding the school and negotiating with the remaining elders and members of the authority. So, they too, were out of question."

"Oh." He paused for a few seconds, contemplating. "Well, did you at least leave a note?"

"To whom?"

"To your mothers (looking at me and Eva) and your father (addressing Nazia)."

"Do you think it would have stayed hidden from our fathers?"

"And the other two spies I have in that house?" I asked.

"And do you think our father cares? We might be burning in front of him, and he won't flinch an eyelid."

"Okay… But from where did you get the money to hire a taxi?"

"We stole from our houses."

"Incredible! I have such lovely thieves and runaways for friends!"

"Shut up."

"Do you want us to leave?"

"So thankless. Shame."

"Let's go, then. Our city boy wouldn't want thieves and runaways in his home."

"Really? 'City boy?' Is that my name now?"

"It's not bad, is it?"

"Not at all!"

"It's true, actually."

"Make all the fun you want. But I know and even you know that you couldn't stay any longer without seeing me."

"That goes both ways, and you know it too."

"Yes. Yes, it does."

"Where are Durga Di and Rihan Bhaiya?"

"Rihan Bhaiya had to leave for the office urgently. Durga Di has gone grocery shopping. But she might not return soon."

"Why?"

"She took up another job recently. It's not permanent. The family who owns all the buildings in this area is very rich. They have two children – one boy and one girl. Both are younger than us. Whenever the parents are not at home, and the maid is on leave, they've asked Durga Di to come over and watch the children. They like her a lot. So, she's their 'on and off' nanny."

"That's what you call her? 'On and off' nanny?" I asked, laughing.

"Yes. Just like I'm the 'city boy.'"

"Fair enough."

We stayed inside for another half hour or so and then went outside to wander around in their locality. Vihaan took us to the common park, where we played with the swings for another hour. Exhausted, we found a large tree in the park and went and sat in its shadow. All we did was talk after that – some of us were lying down with our hands beneath our heads, some had their heads on the other's lap; to change positions, sometimes we'd lean against the tree trunk or against each other.

Around noon, we went back to their house, and Vihaan wrote a small note, addressing Rihan Bhaiya and Durga Di, "I had an amazing day today. Tamanna, Eric, Eva, Nazia and Taheera had come over. No one from the village knows, so don't call home. I am going back with them. I'll be staying with Dadu. Don't worry about me. I feel happy after a long time. I'll see you tomorrow. I love you both."

We took a taxi from the nearest taxi stand and were dropped off at the same taxi stand, which had introduced us to Rahman Uncle. As soon as we got off, we headed towards the common entryway in hurried steps, since it was already dusk and was getting dark.

We reached the entryway in about fifteen minutes, but what met our eyes, could be painted on a canvas with the darkest of shades and colours, and it still wouldn't do justice to the sight that greeted us; the colour, that faded all other colours, was red.

We crossed the threshold, and were venturing closer to what our hearts subconsciously knew, and forbade us from, as though some divine being had climbed down to earth and whispered into our ears a message meant only to be heard by our heartstrings. The road we had traversed on our way out of the village, was now paved with blood-stained pebbles, bloody footprints, and blood puddles. The footprints seemed to be running from everywhere to everywhere, not leaving even a fraction of the ground to breathe; and the blood puddles had formed beside unrecognisable bodies – unrecognisably *dead* bodies. There was one corpse (it was definitely a 'corpse' because there's no way a man could be alive in that condition) which greeted us the instant we had entered, and which had blood flowing, like a river uniting with the ocean, from a skull cracked open by a boulder stone resting on top of the head. Judging by the size of the boulder stone, and the pool of blood that had collected in consequence, the person's skull must have suffered exponentially higher degrees of cracks than was fathomable or even perceivable to our senses. This wasn't the only body we had to sidestep on that path. When we looked up to gauge the magnitude of death staring at us, there were sundry other bodies, all in an assortment. We kept walking through that corridor of death, almost fully aware of what the impending chamber had in store for us.

We crossed another body, lying flat on his back. His eyes were open, and though they were dry, they bore the emotion he must have felt in those last moments when the realisation of his existence's inevitable culmination must have struck him. They were wide open in horror, a horror more or less equivalent to seeing a spectre of doom, of *death*. He had a butcher's knife thrust into his emaciated, sunken stomach, at the very centre. But that probably wasn't the only source behind his painful, untimely farewell. A large stone lay beside his head, smeared in his blood, and one of his hands occupying the other side of his head, was smeared in blood too; the man had most likely received a violent push after being stabbed, to have his head strike the stone. Whether the push was intentional or just a cherry on the murder was immaterial. The result it had engendered, or the contribution it had vouchsafed, could not be reversed. Coincidentally, there was a natural depression on the road a couple of inches away from his head, where his blood, reeking with the helpless ferocity of unfulfilled and ungratified revenge, had formed a tiny reservoir. For a split second, the thought of stooping down and drawing his eyelids over his eyes crossed my mind. It felt cruel to me, that a man, on whom the curtain of death had already fallen, should be left ogling the faint likeness of sequestered life, if that were even possible. But the man, in his immutable tragedy and the ghastly manifestation that the tragedy had presented itself in, had petrified me. I had to be pulled away by Taheera before I could even begin to arrange my thoughts, much rather implement them.

At his feet lay another man, flat on his stomach, with holes in his back. No, these were not holes attributed to repeated stabbing. These were bullet holes. By the sight of it, the man had been shot by a third individual while he was in the process of killing another. His life had been generously sucked out while he was engaged in thoroughly sucking out another's. The gun had made four holes in his back, rendering his *kurta* crimson. There was another stream of blood flowing out of his mouth, conferring a certain amount of redness to the man's otherwise parched lips. This man too, had breathed his last breath holding onto that last, small plausibility of somehow being magically revived to life, or salvaged by Life. Yes, his eyes were open, but the expressions they bore were drastically different from his prey. There was a peculiar realisation in his eyes, the realisation of an idea not completely alien, but one that lingers only in the darker shadow of our minds, the realisation that one might succumb to the same fate that one bestows on the other.

There was a woman a few paces ahead, lying face down, exactly in the middle of the road. She was heavily bull-necked, heavily built, heavily ruptured, and heavily bleeding. There were three bullets accorded to her – one in her lower back on the left, the second on the right side of her waist, and the third on her neck, very close to the head. Her head, dangerously inclined towards her chest, her nose almost touching her bosom, gave it an appearance of being severed from the rest of her body. Her many bangles – red, blue, orange, yellow – all symbolic of her conjugal coexistence, lay on the ground, shattered, as also probably like her family. Her saree had abandoned its function of wrapping her bare body and was partly flailing with the wind, and partly drinking in her blood. A pair of silver *payals*, though blackened with neglected overuse, adorned her plump ankles; at least till the time they could still be referred to as a "pair". Now they were just two separated pieces of jewellery which had adopted independent roles, one of enduring and the other inflicting – the left one, broken, and the right one piercing into her ankle. Her right ankle was also swollen, badly swollen. Such a horrible swelling could not be only attributed to the *payal*; she must have also fractured her ankle in her attempt to safeguard her life.

This phenomenon of guns, bullets, and firing was new to us. We were accustomed to pretty much most weapons which stab or smash, but none which fire. It was difficult for us to wrap our heads around the fact that such a phenomenon existed in our very own hinterland, and also tolerably thrived in our absence.

We passed many more such accursed men and women who had capitulated to their accursed fate and accursed doom, on our way to the convergence of the three villages – the mango tree.

Apart from Dadu, if there was another player that could bring all the people, of all the villages, of all genders, classes, castes, and religions, together, it was the mango tree. That tree was not merely a tree. It was a symbol – of togetherness, friendship, amity and harmony. It was a beacon, like a lighthouse in the middle of an ocean engulfed in dense darkness, besieged by violent tornadoes and storms, and rattled by formidable winds – such was the power of the mango tree, that could show light even to the most estranged. That tree had witnessed innumerable arguments, riots, marriages (mostly coerced, actively, or passively), threats (covert or overt), and a few suicides. But above all, it had witnessed the birth *and* lived through the nurture of a beautiful, and surreal bond between six small children. It had shed tears with them in their predicaments; it had rejoiced with them in their victories; it had given them shelter and provided a benign solace on their darkest days; it had basked in their blithe, although fleeting, joy and exhilaration of childhood days. On the whole, it had lived through their lives as vicariously as the air around them and the dust under their feet; as the moon during early dawn, when the sun rises, and arises with it, the world; as the exhausted traveller in a desert looking at a mirage of people sprawling under the shade of large coconut trees and beside a glistening lake; as the forlorn poet riffling through pages written, but never felt by him.

When we finally reached the mango tree – *our beloved mango tree* – it was gone. No, it had not vanished. It was still there; only that it wasn't standing. It had been severed from a foot above the ground. It was alive no more. An emaciated boy of probably four or five, sat reclined on the tree stock, his head resting on its flat surface, a bullet on his chest. His hair was sweaty and dishevelled, his feet dirty, and his hands muddy. There were more than a few abrasions on his arms and legs, as though he had been running among the tall wheat stalks, whilst clinging on to dear life. The black trails, from the corners of his eyes and on his cheeks, that tears form when rubbed by dirty hands on a dirty face were a clear indication that his last moments were spent crying in anguish. His was a sweet but desperate face – a face not yet ready to welcome or accept death but longing to enjoy life's many treats, a face expecting death to sacrifice him and life to hold on to him like an anchor.

Stretched out from side to side on the fallen bark of the tree, was another man, of not less than sixty. His hair was too white to attest to his age; his forehead too wrinkled, his hands too puckered and his face too hollow. But it was normal in those days for someone to look eighty despite being biologically much less. He had his right arm chopped off from the elbow, and that severed piece of limb lay on the ground, in the shadow of the tree bark, holding a small, ancient-looking pocketknife, with dried blood on its tip. There was a sickle knife too, pinning him by the stomach, not only to the tree bark but also to his death. He looked tired, because below those closed, sleeping eyes, were shadows of long years of relentless hard work and mindless labour. The man was dead, and with him had died all his possible virtues, or vices; his achievements, or failures; his rectitude or decadence. Whether his prolonged life of service had presented him to one of the Gods in heaven, or was he doomed to be withered away in hell under Satan's watch, has always, and will always remain a mystery to me.

These were not the only people – or rather *dead* people – surrounding the perished mango tree. There were hundreds more. I couldn't help but entertain a certain painful inkling of this being only the prelude, and that the real, original story was still to be witnessed. My mind was in a conflict; because no matter how much I tried to keep this notion at bay, it shouldered inside my mind to such a distance, that it infected my ability to reason, and it was all that my mind could think of in that moment.

There were all kinds of people in that chamber of death – different men, women and children, clad in different clothes, dead by different means and at different points of time by different people. But there was still one point of unity among them, and that was *blood*. Suddenly, I felt that I was living the dream that had tormented me all those nights. Once again, the colour *red* was flashing in front of me. I was a passive spectator to the annihilation around me; the frenzied commotion was dead. I did not know what had led to the utter obliteration. I knew that every soul in those three villages was involved. I knew that nobody could see me, because there was no one *left* to see me. I didn't know whether or not there were familiar faces because every face was either distorted, hidden, or bloodied, and the only thought that occupied my mind was of this scene being just the prelude.

"Ouch!" Taheera had slipped… on a puddle of blood. This was the first sound any of us had uttered since our arrival. This monosyllabic sound seemed to reverberate in that deathly sepulchre as though a procession of a dead man had been undertaken by fellow dead beings, to celebrate his advent to the afterlife, with elaborate trumpets, drums and mystical chants.

"Be careful!" Nazia helped Taheera out of the slippery ground. "And *shhh!*"

"Why? Who will hear us? Is anybody even left?" commented Eric. Despite his statement, even he couldn't help but whisper, lest he should disturb the dead.

"What happened here?" asked Taheera, choking. It was evident that she was trying as hard as she could to prevent herself from breaking into a feverish bawl. She too, was probably scared of disturbing the dead.

"Another *danga*," I replied.

"And also, the last one, by the looks of it," added Vihaan.

"What should we do now?" The rest five of us turned to look at the source of this question – Eva. It seems strange that Eva, of all people, would not know what the next step would be, doesn't it? She was the most practical, level-headed and mature member of our lot. But the direst of situations can sometimes do unimaginable things to the unlikeliest of persons.

"Let's check on our families," suggested Vihaan.

"Shouldn't we check on Dadu, Mahira Ma'am, Ashwat Sir and Dr Adam first?" asked Eric.

"No," Nazia replied, curtly.

"Why?"

"Because the knowledge of something terrible happening to them would paralyze us. Do you think we would care enough to check on our families after that?" said Nazia.

"Then, let's go together. All of us," I suggested.

All three villages had frames at their entrances, containing the name of the respective village and that of the district. All three frames had been dislodged from their places and destroyed, their splintered remnants strewn everywhere, as broken, as fractured as they could be. In any of the three villages, there was not a single being breathing, not a single chest heaving, not a single pair of eyes wandering, not a single finger twitching, not a single heart beating. There were dead bodies everywhere, and there was not an inch of the ground which their blood had not gilded. No matter where I turned my head, no matter in which direction, blood had lodged itself as a permanent guest in my eyes. I can't remember a single green leaf or the tiny *shiuli* flowers that marked our villages in those months. Even if there were, my mind never grasped them. The death was too oppressive. The few concrete houses, belonging to the rich landlords and tax collectors, were not spared either. Broken, crushed, and burnt; there were very few walls which still stood erect. These walls, although fortunate enough to not be vandalised, had been badly defaced with the refrain 'BURN IN HELL' written boldly in blood.

All the communal places – places of worship, shops, postal offices – had been desecrated either in flames or in blood. Outside the postal offices, there were heaps and heaps of letters burnt, or burning, to ashes. In the entire course of that day, watching those letters burn still remains one of my gloomiest memories. Letters, usually, contain the heart and soul of the writer; they contain the anguish of the ailing father writing to his son in the city for some extra cash because his monsoon crops failed, and he had to repay his debts, and buy medicines for his cancer inflicted wife; they contain the feigned optimism of the prematurely married daughter, writing with blistered hands, scraped fingers and bruised, tear-filled eyes, about the wonders and luxuries of city life, her husband's kindness and her in-laws' hospitality; they contain the sweet lies of the tired, dejected son, scourging for employment and livelihood in an overpopulated city, writing to his mother about how large cities are rightly called 'wish-granters,' and how his decision of pursuing his dream could not have been more correct; they contain the selfless tears of a desolate mother, widowed at the ripe age of twenty-six after bearing five children, writing to her oldest daughter in the United States of America, about how content she felt with all her children busy in their successful lives, and how she now sought to be united with her Creator; they contain the soaring aspirations of the youngest brother writing to his eldest sister in the civil services, about how fascinated he is by the sky and the stars, the moon and the sun, the clouds and the rain, and how eager he was to snatch one of the many stars that his sky held, style it into a pendant, and gift it to his mother; they contain the dwindling aspirations of the youngest and only sister of five elder brothers, writing a string of complaints to her oldest brother about how she felt she were never born, how she felt like a burden, how much she hated her parents and her village, how much she longed to break free, how much she had started contemplating over the possibility of her death and how she was finally going to effect it.

But we dared not stop to imbibe the actual destruction that had besieged us; one halt and all the courage that we had summoned would have drowned in the blood around us.

We made for my and Vihaan's family first and entered the first death chamber. Once we crossed the line on which the frame had earlier stood, I was hit by a stifling, damp wave of air on my face. I don't know if it was just a figment of my imagination, but it did suffocate me.

Ultimately, after what seemed like a long, tedious walk, we came face-to-face with the house which I had come to despise over the years.

There was not a soul inside. We checked all the rooms, cupboards, shelves, under the table, and every possible place which could cover a human being, but in vain.

"Come outside," Eric said with a grim face.

"What? Why?" I asked.

"I was looking outside while all of you were busy here."

"And?"

"And you need to come outside and see for yourself!" Eric replied with an odd urgency. There was something in his voice that made me weak in the knees. A lingering panic was trying to hide itself behind the calm, carefree visage that he always assumed. He had seen something, and it had taken him almost his entire resolve and strength to inform us about it.

We went after him to the back of the house. There was a fresh stream of blood flowing parallelly to the side wall. A closer and steadier look revealed not just one, but four, six, or seven streams! Vihaan and I clutched each other's hands because we had a foreboding of whom those seven streams might belong to. After a point, the two of us weren't walking; we were dragging and pulling each other. We were trying to support each other when there was not an ounce of strength that we could muster for ourselves.

Our final step disclosed seven bodies in two heaps – four and three in each, respectively. The first one had my father as the base, whose head had been severed, with only a thin piece of flesh joining it to his neck. On top of him lay my grandmother, with a twisted ankle and a crushed, profusely bleeding forehead. Lying face up on her, was Vihaan's mother. She had been lacerated across the body, starting from her left shoulder, down to her right lower abdomen. Surmounting the heap was Vihaan's father. I could locate no visible injury to him, except a long sword, piercing through him, all the way down to my father. So long was the sword, and so deep had it been impaled that only its hilt could be seen; not even the cross-guard was spared the bitter taste of human blood. What were Vihaan's parents doing in my house? I never knew…

The second mound began with Rahul Bhaiya at the bottom; both his arms were burnt and there was a purple mark running all through the visible part of his neck. Above him, was my second brother, Naveen; his mouth, an overwhelming bowl of blood and broken teeth. I couldn't detect any other injury in him, except a terribly twisted ankle. Finally, topping this mound, was my mother, her saree nothing but a soggy piece of red clothing. There were long, deep abrasions all over her – on either side of her neck; running haywire along both the arms and feet; slicing both her cheeks. None of these wounds – either in Rahul Bhaiya, or Naveen or Ma – were lethal; and yet, there was no chance on earth that they were alive when we reached them because they had met their fate in exactly the same way as the former group – a long, broad sword piercing through all three of them.

"They make swords like these?" I asked, barely opening my mouth, barely thinking.

"Let's go," Eva whispered in my ears. Frozen, I didn't move an inch, nor did I pay any heed to Eva. I stood there, transfixed, glued, horrified, numbed. All my life, I had detested everyone in those two mounds with all my heart, except for my mother. There was no chance that those people could be worthy of my sympathy or compassion or tears. But my mother? She had to endure the mortification of not only spending most part of her pliant life in the company and clutches of those monsters but also die with them. She was never given the dignity that she deserved in her life, nor did she ever ask for it; and so, even Death did not deem it important enough to grant her a tiny grain of dignity. After a while, I forgot about everyone there, and the only face that remained in my mind was that of my mother. I didn't just lose my mother that day; I lost my chance of ever having one last conversation with her, one last hug, one last smile, one last truth…

Taheera closed into Nazia and clutched her arm tightly the second we turned at the roundabout and stood facing their house. From the outside, it seemed that the house had been granted unsolicited mercy. Even the latch on the door was intact, except for a bloody hand mark. We pushed it open and entered, only to find the house in utter disarray. They had been robbed. The kitchen had almost entirely been stripped naked – utensils, spices, grain, oil, vegetables, fruits, cereals – not a single object remained. They had coveted all the furniture, curtains, carpets, and every other item that could either be sold in a flea market or used for personal luxury.

Without wasting too much time thinking about objects which seemed missing, or about the nakedness of the house, we entered the room which had sheltered the 'man of the house'. To reduce this man to a corpse, it had taken just two clicks of the gun – not a click more, not a click less. Two bullets, one on the forehead, and the other towards the left of his chest were enough to snap whatever little life had remained, and weakly lingered, in him after his fateful day. But unlike the wretched misery that was outside of this house, the inside felt peaceful, especially their father's face. He was lying on his cot, eyes closed, and mouth shaped in a smile, as though in a final attempt at flouting his disability.

"Are you okay?" I asked Nazia, pulling at her elbow. Her face seemed like a barren surface, bereft of any emotions. She was staring at her dead father intently, but there was something about her demeanour that betrayed to me an inner struggle, a deep conundrum.

"I don't know. He looks so content… Does he really deserve such an easy death? There is no doubt about how much he had to endure these past few months, yet I don't feel any remorse or pity for him, nor am I happy that he is finally free. I don't know what or how to *feel*. All I know is that he doesn't deserve to be happy… Not even in his death."

Our next destination was the twins' house. By now, our eyes and ears had gotten accustomed to crackling red and orange flames. These flames were everywhere, climbing houses, trees, cowsheds, and shops, engulfing the living and non-living alike. Probably this was the reason why it took us a while to identify or locate their house. It was up in flames too. The surrounding trees, the bushes, the wooden fence around their house, their tiny, black shop – my eyes seemed like windows that opened only to fire.

"How do we find your parents?" asked Vihaan, glancing toward Eva and Eric.

"There is no way we can find them now. Either they are in there – in which case, there is not a chance in hell that they would still be breathing – or they must have fled," replied Eric.

"We can't even ask anyone. There is not a single living soul anywhere around," said Taheera in a sad, helpless voice.

"How bad is it to not be able to feel anything?" Eva asked, staring into the blazing fire. "My house is burning, and I have no clue whether my parents are alive or dead. Still, I don't feel sad. I don't even know if that is the right emotion for this moment. How horrible a person does this make me?"

"You are not a horrible person," I said, taking her arm in mine, and resting my head on her shoulder. That was the only consolation I could offer her.

"You are not alone, Eva," Nazia reassured, curling her fingers through Eva's. "You are not alone."

As our last and only resort to find their parents, we decided to check the hospital. We assumed that people, no matter how seriously wounded, must have made for the hospital. We had expected to see a larger-than-normal commotion there, with nurses and administrators and doctors, all running around in a confused frenzy. We had reasons to believe that Dr Adam too, would be busy tending to all the patients and reviving the little life left in the most pitiful. But all our assumptions and hopes crumbled to the barren ground when we saw the hospital building ablaze against the dark grey sky, with bodies, bleeding and parched, skewed in its courtyard. The rioters had not pardoned even the hospital.

But there was one body unmistakably identifiable – Dr Adam's. Two bullets – one on the forehead, and the other close to the heart – had managed to suck his soul and snatch him away from a place that was beating on his pulse. His blood-soaked white shirt had turned scarlet, and he lay lifeless on the ground with his left leg twisted backwards from the knee, and his eyes gaping wide open.

With no other means left to locate the missing pair of parents, we finally made our way to Dadu's shop.

The shop was nothing less than a blackened dilapidation. It had been reduced to half its original glory and was still burning when we reached it. All the boxes, big and small, the drinks, packets of chips, the tiny containers of chewing gums and chocolates, the oil and water bottles, and other essential and non-essential items – not a single article had been spared. The fire, burning on every inch, every particle of that shop, was crackling with a vehemence unparalleled to even the darkest pits of Hell. I looked towards the river, to see if there was any way we could pour its water on the shop. But it could not be possible. In my stupor, what I had overlooked, were trails of blood, all leading to the river. It was no more a river, but a bloody deluge of floating scarred, seared, warped, shot, cut, dead bodies. It was crimson with bodies afloat as far as my eyes could reach.

I turned to look at the school, but it too had met the same fate as the hospital, the shop and the entire village.

Enveloped in a thick, opaque blanket of fire and smoke, it had been annihilated from its core. We ventured closer to the school to try and see if there was anyone inside whom we could save. But the fire was too dense to allow even the smallest hole for us to peek through.

Dazed, I moved towards the river, unaware of what I intended to find there. But I did find it. I did find what my mind was looking for and what my heart was resisting. I found the bodies of Dadu, Ashwat Sir and Mahira Ma'am; blood-soaked, charred, and disfigured.

Dadu's face was beyond recognition. It had required just one blow on the head to crack open his skull. I could only identify him with his white clothes, although stained, and wrinkled, arthritic hands. Whoever had killed him, and whoever had dragged him to the river's shore, had not cared enough to close his eyes and mouth.

Ashwat Sir lay just below Dadu. It wasn't difficult to identify him, since he and Dr Adam were the only people in the village who used to wear formals – ironed shirts and crisp trousers. But his attire had all but melted into his skin. Not an inch of him remained uninjured, unbloodied, or uncharred.

It would have been impossible to identify Mahira Ma'am, had she and Sir not been holding hands. She had been stripped naked of every piece of clothing, and there were still small patches of dancing fire spread all over her body. Her body had shrivelled, with some parts already forming ashes. It struck me as strange initially that her body had started decaying and had yet retained small pockets of fire scattered. But it was Nazia who pointed out how meticulously and vindictively her life had been cut short; there was a can of glycerine lying beside her, an empty can.

The last time we had witnessed a similar sight, it had brought me to my knees, bawling, like a baby crying for the safety of her mother's embrace, for the familiarity and protection of an eternal refuge. But it was not so this time. The reliving of past horror, the culmination of a long-held dream, the crashing down of the faintest ray of hope I didn't know I had, and the end of the lives of four stars who had entered this world with the sole purpose of making it a better place, a more beautiful place… it makes one too tired to cry, too awake to faint, too stunned to fall on the ground, too paralysed to express, and too numb to feel.

Mindlessly, we strolled back to the mango tree, to whatever had remained of our childhood motif. There was no other place for us to resort to, no other place that our minds were accustomed to. But at that moment, even the mango tree seemed alien; unrecognisable. A world utterly annihilated, and *dead,* had been thrust on us – a world that none of us were ready to witness or endure. It was doing everything in its power to create in our hearts the desolation that it had itself been subjected to. But what was it that prevented the germination of hatred, bitterness and resentment for the people we had grown up with and around? What was it that was blocking the doors to a lifetime of dreadful anguish? Was it strength? Was it the chasm that we had created between ourselves and our environment? Was it the resolution of never allowing the rancour that surrounded us, to touch us? Or was it plain, simple love that we had chosen over hatred? I don't know...

"Where do we go from here?" Eric asked when we were just a few paces away from the tree.

"Look at the sky. It's going to start raining soon. Let's go to the city and see if we find some shelter there," Vihaan suggested.

"NOBODY IS GOING ANYWHERE!"

We swerved around to see where the voice was coming from. There were three huge, bulky men standing a couple of yards behind us, with long, polished but blood-stained lathis and rusty daggers. With their faces, clothes and hands covered in blood splashes, they resembled, at the very least, brutes, savages and monsters. Their eyes boiling with an uncontrollable compulsion to kill, their teeth clenched, and bodies poised in a readiness to attack, they pounced on us with their lathis. Fortunately, we succeeded in dodging all three of them without a scrape. But that just seemed to add more fuel to their fury. Eric and I managed to pick up a boulder each, while the others collected smaller rocks and some heavy sticks, and prepared for a defence.

There was no chance of us actively fighting those men; they towered over us even from a distance. So, we thought of disarming them and then running away as fast as our little legs would allow us. There were three men, so we divided ourselves into three groups of two each – Eric and me, Vihaan and Taheera, and Nazia and Eva. The man who charged at me and Eric was carrying a dagger. The moment we felt that he was close enough, we threw a rock aiming at his face. It hit him between his eyes, just below the temple. That was sufficient to momentarily thwart him. I ran ahead with a large boulder and struck him on the hand in which he had been holding the dagger. As he dropped it, Eric immediately picked it up and threatened him with it. But the man was unrelenting. He took a couple of steps forward and punched Eric, throwing him on the ground. Without caring less about his dagger, he redirected himself towards me. *'No, there is no way I'll allow this man to get hold of me…'* was the only refrain in my head. I was a bit too far off from Eric to be able to pick up the dropped dagger. I had nothing to protect myself, nothing to attack him with. Instead, I ran. I scurried away towards the tall bushes, frantically attempting to trick him into losing me. But he was persistent in his pursuit of me. After running for a couple of minutes or so, he caught up to me, held my arm, pulled me towards him, and slapped me with all the strength that his hefty body could gather. I fell to the ground, unconscious.

I don't know what happened to me during that period when I lost consciousness. But when I was restored to my senses, I could feel a throbbing pain between my thighs, below the abdomen, at or near my vagina. Eva held my hand throughout the distance from the bushes to the entrance to our district. On the other side, was Nazia, who too, trudged very close alongside me. Just behind me was Vihaan, walking very close. Eric and Taheera were leading our tiny procession. A quarter of an hour had passed before I realised that I was wet between the thighs. I looked down to see what it was, but I didn't find any water. Instead, my frock was red, soaking *red.*

19

ANOTHER TIME, ANOTHER PLACE

We bid adieu to our villages and re-entered the world of the city. The clouds had been pouring heavily on us for the past ten to fifteen minutes, and the sight that we encountered on entering the city made it harder for us to differentiate between the two adjacent worlds.

Walking aimlessly and listlessly, we dragged ourselves through the pools, left by the torrential rain that had swept our district and the city, choking the roads. I had always imagined the world of the cities to be in stark contrast to our miserable village life. But that day, even my somnolent conscience could not help but notice a few vague similarities – heavy downpours never dampened industrious spirits; groups of men sitting under the shade of small tea shops and sipping *chai* from a *kulhad*; trees destroying our mud and straw huts, and trees plummeting down on stationary buildings and cars; children dancing around with their friends gleefully, with their mothers scolding and chasing them; the pleasant, musky petrichor impregnating the air; the dalliance between the shy tree leaves and the strong winds; the grey clouds swarming the vast, desolate sky; and us.

Meandering through the noisy bustle, the dense traffic, and sundry puddles, we entered a busy marketplace. It was too crowded, the kind in which you can see the five strands of grey hair on a young mother's head, you can feel people's sweaty hands rub against yours and hear their heavy breathing in your ears. We held each other's hands as tightly as we could to avoid getting jostled away. But sadly, it wasn't enough. A fire broke out in a small furniture shop, and it didn't require even the blink of an eye to engulf the shop in its tentacles. The fire did not spread to the adjoining shops because of the rain but soon consumed the interior. Even before anyone could think of controlling the fire or rescuing the inhabitants of the shop, the crowd had broken into a frenzy. Everyone was running everywhere. Some with toddlers in their arms, some with bags full of vegetables and fruits, some trying to protect their newly bought, second-hand phones and laptops, and others just heedlessly shoving everyone out of their way. In that mayhem, I don't recall how or when I let go of Vihaan's hand and got separated from them. I kept pushing myself around in the attempt to find them somewhere – maybe hidden inside a shop, or sitting on the tiny stairs in front of shops, or maybe on the ground, fallen, trying to stand up. Like a maniac, I kept darting around, yelling my throat soar.

I stopped when I reached the end of that marketplace. The crowd had waned away, with very few lingering shadows. I stood under a small tree to get a better perspective, at a last, desperate attempt to locate them. But I couldn't…

Weeping, I went towards the closest shop and sat down beside it. But I was kicked out the instant the shopkeeper saw a potential customer turn away from the shop after noticing a miserable, piteous girl in a red-stained frock, rocking back and forth, clutching her arms and sobbing vehemently. In a trance, I started walking, unknowing of where I was headed. When I reached that unfortunate shop, I heard women discussing the fiasco – "You know, they found half a cigarette on the heap of wooden waste. Oh, and they had that tiny shelf too where they'd keep the idols and *Meera* would habitually show the incense stick around them and in the shop. I heard that the incense stick had fallen out of its case as well."

I continued on that endless path till it was dark and the moon was lurking behind the clouds. The rain had slowed down to an unsure drizzle, and there was barely any activity on the street. My mind felt as dark as the night, and that throbbing pain between my thighs had still not receded. I kept walking, unconscious of where I was going or whom I was passing, till I saw a tiny shop across the road, resembling that of Dadu's. A lone man with hair as white as chalk and a moustache the size of a baby caterpillar, possibly the owner, was sitting on one of the lower shelves, leaning against a cardboard, smoking an almost finished cigarette. I scampered to the shop, unheeding the few motor vehicles that were still haunting that road.

"Can I have something to eat?" I requested in an undertone. That was the highest volume that my throat allowed. I couldn't raise it higher even if I wanted to.

The man examined me from top to bottom. His eyes lingered for a few moments on the red patch on my dress, before coming back to my face.

"Take whatever you want. There's a stool there you can sit on. Bring it here if you don't want to further wet yourself," he replied indifferently.

"I don't have any money," I muttered, apologetically.

"Did I ask for it? Just do as I say," he replied, curtly.

I complied and grabbed a packet of chips hanging from the roof on a thread.

I was busy gobbling the packet of chips when the shopkeeper turned on the radio…

"Aaj agar bhar aayi hain

Boondein baras jaayengi

Kal kya pata inke liye

Aankhein taras jaayengi

Jaane kab ghum hua, kaha khoya

Ek ansoon chhupaake rakha tha…"

[If they have welled up today,

Tears will shower,

Who knows if tomorrow

My eyes will yearn for them,

I don't know when they were lost, or where,

But I had kept a teardrop hidden.]

20

A NEW WORLD

After filling myself with the packet of chips, I thanked the shopkeeper and started walking once again. I kept on my track until I spotted a bungalow. It was massive. The moonlight shone on its slanted roof, illuminating the curtained windows of the two rooms on the top floor. There were two more floors, but the night barred me from discerning their size or if they were open. I noticed a small gazebo not far from the bungalow. '*That's probably theirs too... Must be very rich...*' The house and the gazebo were enclosed by a brick wall, with just one gate facing the main road. I ventured closer to the gate and to my relief, it was ajar, just enough for me to get in. There was a security guard too, but he was sleeping, snoring. I sneaked in without disturbing the gate or the sleeping man, and headed straight for the gazebo, not bothering to look anywhere else.

The rainwater had formed tiny puddles on the grass, and I had to be wary of not stepping on the puddles and a wilful splash waking up the guard. The gazebo had a beautiful bulb hanging from its roof with fireflies humming around its flickering light. As I inched closer, and my eyes got accustomed to the light, I saw that it was a well-maintained garden that had adorned the gazebo. I couldn't identify the flowers because it was too dark and

I had no intention of exploring the garden, but I could still discriminate between the immense variety. '*Stop looking... There is nothing flowery in your life right now...*' I remember telling myself.

There were two long benches in the gazebo facing each other. I curled myself up on the drier one and closed my eyes to enter a night-long dream of blood pouring from different people, from different parts of their bodies. It was the same dream, only this time, I could recognise the people – our neighbours, acquaintances (pleasant and the not-so-pleasant), friends, foes, relatives, my friends' families and my own. The commotion was there too, but it was muted, without any voice. It was a silent commotion, like that of people who have ascended beyond the realm of living voices.

"Ramu! Ramu!"

"Who is this girl, sleeping here? How did you even let her enter?"

"I…I didn't, Sir."

"Oh, wow! You were not even aware that a stranger had entered the house? Please tell me exactly what we are paying you for?"

"I am sorry, Sir. I was extremely tired yesterday. I hadn't slept at all in the last couple of days. You know about my wife's…"

"Yes, yes, I know. But that is not my problem. I don't give a damn if you're tired or if your wife is dying. What I do give a damn about is my money. And my family's security, of course. You managed to jeopardise both. Please leave."

"I am sorry, Sir."

"And don't come back."

Exactly three months after the day he was dismissed, his wife's breasts heaved their last, strained sigh. She had been diagnosed with metastatic breast cancer, a month before her husband's dismissal, which had spread to her lungs and bones too. They consulted a doctor when, at the age of fifty-five, her husband felt charged with a sudden, unexpected virility at three in the morning, and pulled off his sleeping wife's nightgown, only to be aghast at her unusually swollen, lumpy left breast. After her diagnosis, he asked his employer for a loan, scrouging at the tiny rays of hope that the doctor had led them to see. The loan was denied, and a month later, his services too. I was given these particulars by Veda.

Veda was the only daughter and the youngest member of that household, older than me by three years.

"What do we do with this girl?" "This girl" was half asleep.

"Let's at least wake her up. She has been sleeping on our property for God knows how long. Hey! Wake up!"

I was woken up by violent jerks and harsh tones. When asked for my name and where I had come from, I could not reply; I had lost my voice to the rain and my excessive crying. I stared at them open-mouthed. I could hear voices, shouts rather, but nothing made sense. Far from forming any response, my brain felt too weak to even process the words. I felt paralysed, frozen; physically and mentally. I looked around – a man and a woman were standing right in front of me, yelling; there were two children sitting on the steps that led into the house; there was an old lady, in a particularly faded, navy-blue saree, standing not far away from the children, but far enough to denote an unspoken, impassable distance. My eyes lingered on her for a few seconds before I uttered, "Tamanna."

"What? Be louder, girl!" the man standing in front of me yelled.

"Tamanna," I replied in a strained whisper.

"She is so stubborn!" the woman remarked.

"She won't be for long," the man said in an angry hush. He clutched my arm with a vehemence that reminded me of my father, and asked, "What is your name?"

"Can't you two see that she is sick? She is whispering not because she is stubborn but because she is sick! Her hair is wet; obviously, she got wet in the rain last night. Shyam, leave her arm," the old lady instructed. She was standing beside me by then with one of her arms around my shoulder, her frail hand strong on my weak shoulder. She had started pulling me along with her towards the house when the man asked, "Where are you taking her?"

"Inside the house."

"She will not enter my house."

"I'll take her to my room."

"She will not step through that door."

"And why should I listen to you?"

"Because it's my house."

"No; it's my husband's house. He isn't dead yet." With that, she took me inside the house.

The house seemed much larger from the inside than from the outside. Upon entering through the door, we entered the living room. All the walls in this room were a light shade of beige, except the main wall which had a wallpaper with symmetrical floral prints in light blue, pink and lavender. The living room had three sofas aligned adjacent to each other, one carpet in the centre on which there was a moderately sized centre-table, and an enormous wall-unit facing the sofas which contained a television, a few shelves decorated with tiny figurines, cabinets containing CD's and albums, and some small potted indoor plants. There was another wooden wall-unit, separating the living room from the kitchen and dining area. A flight of stairs was attached to this wall unit, and we went upstairs. The other wall adjoining the stairs had the same wallpaper as the main wall of the living room.

We reached the next floor after what seemed like ages. *'This old lady is pretty old...'* There were two rooms there (their house had a total of four rooms – one downstairs, which I missed the first time I entered because it was on the opposite end of the house from the kitchen; two upstairs; one on the top-most floor. This last one, most likely built as a servant-quarter, because it was almost detached from the rest of the house and was on the terrace, was my room for the next eight years). One, immediately on the left, and the other on the right, at the end of a short corridor. There was a 'lobby area' (as they had christened it) too, containing another television unit and a sofa facing it. The old lady took me to the room on the left.

An old, senile man, nearly a skeleton, was sleeping in the room, lying flat on his back. He looked too weak to even sit up or talk or eat. The flesh on his bones had wrinkled like crumbled paper, and the room had a strange, foul smell to it.

"I want to adopt this girl," the old lady said to the old man.

"What?" the old man asked, barely audible and barely opening his lips.

"I want to take in this girl," she reiterated, a bit louder this time.

"Which girl?" he asked without opening his eyes.

"You'll see which girl if you open your eyes," she replied sternly.

"Old age has done nothing to your tongue, woman. It's still as sharp. Go away. Don't disturb me."

The old lady walked over to his bed, pulling me alongside her. Glaring down at him, she said, "Open your eyes, and listen to what I am saying."

He finally complied. "What is it?"

"I want to adopt this girl. I want her to live with us, with me."

He looked at me for a few seconds, from top to bottom, and proceeded to ask, "I've never seen this girl. Who is she?"

"Tamanna."

"Tamanna who?"

"A girl. Maybe ten years of age, or eleven."

"Do we know her?"

"No."

"Why do you want to adopt her?"

"Because she needs me… and I need her too."

"Do whatever you want. Don't trouble me." With that, he turned over. "Close the door when you leave."

"This girl" was later inducted into the family and became their "adopted daughter." This family consisted of Mukeshlal, his wife Sheela, their son and daughter-in-law Shyam and Bina respectively, and their two children, Veda and Lakshman. My foster parents, Bina and Shyam, and the patriarch of the family, Mukeshlal, were against it. But Mukeshlal was a senile, ninety-year-old man. So, when his wife, Sheela, implored him to allow "the girl" a seat at the family dinner table, he found protesting her wish too onerous. Eventually, the government records too christened me as their "adopted ward." But neither the seat at the dinner table nor my name in the government records enabled me a route into the hearts of those people; not that I made any effort to construct such a route. But there was one person who succeeded at constructing a route to my heart, from whom I failed at divorcing myself – Sheela Dadi.

Sheela Dadi married into the family at the age of twelve, just after transitioning from being a "girl" to a "lady." Her husband was fifteen years older, with an active, uncontrolled libido, a product of his youth, as explained to Sheela Dadi by her mother-in-law. Sheela Dadi's mother-in-law would grace her with a vain, presumptuous smile each time she complained of soreness or walked in a noticeably absurd gait. Sheela Dadi had her first son when she was slightly above thirteen. He was born premature and died within the first hour of his birth. They went on to have five sons and four daughters, out of which, two could not cross the first-month limit and three died before puberty. Unfortunately, the remaining children were three girls and one boy. This boy was Shyam. Sheela Dadi had no sense of attachment to her family or the world in general. Her children were brought up spoilt by their grandparents; the daughters were given away in marriage in succession during their teens, and the son took no time to don his father's clothes. Sheela Dadi had no contribution to the household except serving all its members. Her detachment was not only reciprocated by the family but also replicated by the youngest generation – her grandchildren. Veda and Lakshman feared their father, scorned their mother, ignored but obliged their grandfather, and treated their grandmother the way everyone treated the house helps. Nor did Sheela Dadi ever attempt to bond with her children; she knew it would be a practice in vain. So, she jumped at the first opportunity to salvage her receding humanity and compassion when she saw a girl of an impressionable age in a vulnerable state physically, mentally, and circumstantially.

The next eight years of my life became another hazy task at survival. There are tiny snippets of this second phase which I have carefully preserved in my memory. Carefully, because these eight years were the darkest and most obscure years of my life. If there ever shone a sun over me, I never saw it; if there were stars and moon glistening over me, I never appreciated them; if there were ever little birds chirping around me, I never heard them; if there were ever children gleefully laughing and playing around me, I never perceived it; if there were ever flowers blooming around me, I never looked at them; if there was ever any music in the air around me, it never touched me. I had built an impenetrable pall around myself, a black curtain that never allowed itself to slide or fall. But this curtain did not make me completely unreceptive to my surroundings. There were certain elements that were powerful enough – or were given power enough – to seep through the pall. Dark clouds of an overcast sky, dried, colourless leaves of an old tree, moaning paupers and their cadaverous children, my foster parents' slight innuendos, and gradually, their blatant, unabashed disparagements.

My first encounter with Veda and Lakshman happened within ten days of my arrival.

"When are you leaving?" I was in my room, sitting on my bed and reading, when Veda came in.

"What?"

"I asked you when you are leaving."

"I don't know."

"Do you like staying here?"

"Not in the least."

"Then why are you still here?"

"Because I have nowhere else to be."

"If you did, would you leave our house?"

"Gladly."

"Do you hate us?"

"Not all of you."

"Why?"

"Why not?"

"I don't know." She came in and sat on my bed.

"Hasn't your mother forbidden you from talking to me?"

"Yes, but she isn't home right now. I can talk to you as long as she doesn't find out."

"Why do you want to talk to me?"

"Because I have no one else to talk to."

"You have your brother."

"He barely steps out of his room."

"Talk to Sheela Dadi."

"About what?"

"I don't know. Maybe what you did in school."

"She wouldn't understand. She's illiterate."

"Whatever. I don't think talking to *me* is the wisest idea."

"Do you not like me?"

"I need to know you to decide whether I like you or not."

"We are almost the same age, yet I don't get half of what you say."

"I thought you go to school."

"I do!"

"Then? Do you not read?"

"Read what?"

"Books!"

"Why would I read books?"

"What else do you do in your free time?"

"I play and watch cartoons and movies."

"Oh."

"What do you do?"

"I used to play. I still read."

"Whom did you play with? Your friends?"

"Yes."

"Where are they now?"

"I don't know."

"Why did you leave them?"

"I didn't leave them! I got lost!"

"Don't yell at me!"

"Don't ask personal questions!"

"You're so rude! Why are you even here? This isn't your house! Go back to your dirty village!"

"What is going on here?" Lakshman was standing at the door.

"Can you please take your sister away from here?" I glared at him.

"Veda, what are you doing here? Do you not remember how firm Ma was about not talking to this girl?"

"I was getting bored! So, I came to talk to her! I wanted to know why Ma called her a whore!"

"Called me a *what*?" I asked her in disbelief.

"A *whore*! I don't even know what that means! I wanted to ask you, but you started yelling at me before that!"

"Why did she call me that?" I was almost in tears.

"She said people like you and from your social background are always involved in this business, and that your frock was red when we found you," Veda replied.

"Veda!" Lakshman entered the room and clutched her by the arm. "Why can't you keep shut for once? Go to your room right now!" And he pushed her towards the door. Veda ran to her room, bawling. He turned to me, and pointing a finger at me, said, "Stay away from my sister. She is very naïve. I don't want her to mix with the likes of you."

One day (I had turned almost fourteen by then), when I was in my room – the one constructed to be the servant's quarter – Bina barged in, yelling at the top of her voice.

"You spend the entire day in this room! What on earth did we bring you in for?"

"That's my question too – why did you bring me in?"

"I keep asking myself the same question, but I never seem to reach at an answer."

"Perhaps I have."

"What?"

"You wanted a slave."

"What?"

"Yes, you wanted a slave. Another lesser-than-human being who would toil for you, slog for you and live unhesitatingly under your feet."

"How dare you?"

"How dare I? Why? Do you have any other answer? Was I wrong? I'd love to be corrected."

"You are a blithering, moronic, thankless bitch who deserves to be left on the street for the wild dogs and men like those who had raped you."

This was followed by my shoe that I hurled at her, pushing her out of my room and locking myself inside it. I could hear Bina bawling and whining about me to her children and to Sheela Dadi for the next couple of hours. She thanked her stars for obedient and submissive children like Veda and Lakshman and accused Sheela Dadi of the "difficult times" that had befallen them since my adoption. She repeated the whole story, with the same details and a higher degree of drama, to her husband when he returned from his office in the evening. Shyam tried to unlock my room, but I had locked the latch. When he gave up, he instructed everyone in the house, including the maids, to not give me any food till I apologised to Bina.

Late at night, when everyone was asleep, Sheela Dadi came knocking on my door with some food. I opened the door for her and let her in.

"Dadi, why did you adopt me? You knew nothing except my name when you asked Mukeshlal about me. Why did you do that?" I asked her once I was done eating.

"Because I had seen what the others hadn't seen, and didn't see, until after I told them, much later – the blood stain on your frock. I knew instantly what had happened, what you had gone through."

"How did you know?"

"Because I had gone through it too; in a different way, though. The ten children that I birthed, including the one who was born premature, were, and are, children born out of force. I was never introduced to Shyam's father before I was married off to him. The first time I saw his face, was on the day of our *suhagaraat*. I still remember that face as vividly as though I am seeing it in front of me right now. There was a strange hysteria on his face, a madness. He was excited like a child looking at a soft toy, but a child's excitement is innocent; it's artless. His wasn't. There was malice and hostility beneath that excitement, an apparent nonchalance for the object of excitement. A child loves a soft toy, she will care for it and keep it safe. She will handle the soft toy with the sensitivity and concern of a mother handling her baby. She will make sure that no harm is ever done to the soft toy. But Shyam's father…his excitement was diluted by hunger and power. He was hungry to devour his soft toy, and he knew that he possessed the power to do so easily, without any real resistance. He didn't care for his soft toy; all he cared about was satisfying his hunger. Whatever happened to the soft toy – whether it got torn up or not, whether it was in pain or not, whether it cried or not, whether it screamed in agony or not, whether it felt scared or not, whether it wished to be dead or not – were not his concerns." She took a brief pause, and continued after a few seconds, "This happened every night, except on days when he was particularly tired, or I seemed less ravishing, or somebody else had already quenched his thirst. The very first week of our marriage had instilled in me a fear and disgust: fear because each night of that first week, I'd lose the sense of who or what I was; I'd lose myself to him, physically and mentally, and no matter how much I cried or begged, he would always succeed in snatching me away from myself. Disgust, because he would do all sorts of things to me that I could never imagine doing to anyone, things that make me shiver even when I think of them now."

"There used to be a mirror on the wall adjacent to our bed, and I remember looking at it, lying prostrate, with him sitting on me and shaking vigorously, and a constant, ever-increasing pain in my bottom. I used to be naked during these hours; there was nothing to cover me. And I'd look at the image in the mirror, just look at it, and feel nothing. Absolutely nothing, except that pain. The face that stared back at me, was dead. There is no second way of describing that face. Dead."

"After a few months, maybe nearly a year, it became routine. He'd start with his business, and I'd start with mine –thinking about the next day's chores. I'd think of what I'd cook for breakfast, lunch and dinner, which saree I'd wear the following morning, which suit he'd wear to office the next day, which vegetables and fruits I had to buy, perfecting my *dal* because I had been scolded for not adding enough salt; I'd think about how many torn sarees

I had to replace and the budget, about the milkman's wife who hadn't returned from her *maika* in over a month, about a girl from a nearby school who had killed herself and a boy from our locality who had become an IPS officer; I remember thinking that if I ever had children, I'd want boys and not girls because girls kill themselves and boys become IPS officers. I remember wondering during one such night if I'd kill myself too…"

"No one told me that I was leading the life of a slave, that I was unknowingly providing services and receiving nothing in return. I used to look down upon a woman in our area who was a prostitute; I'd abhor her. But it took me a lifetime to realise that the woman I had scorned with such vehemence, was leading a better life than I did. Yes, her job involved pain sometimes, often coupled with a degree of helplessness, but she was paid in return for that! At least, she was benefitting from all the pain and vulnerability and weakness. Despite being in pain, she had power. She had power over the men who came to her; she had power over providing them or not providing them with the services they were so desperate for. Was I being paid for my services? No. Was I benefitting from my pain? No. Did I have power over the man who was desperate for my services? No. The woman earned her money herself; she worked for it. Did I earn any money for myself? No. I took whatever Shyam's father gave me."

"I used to consider her as the lowest being. But she wasn't. I was."

"How did you know that you were being wronged?" I asked.

"The woman; the prostitute, Meena. She told me. I met her in the marketplace one day when I had gone to buy some vegetables. And of course, I tried to hide from her and sneak off to some other vendor. But she saw me, pulled me towards her and hugged me. She had always been very kind to me. I still don't know why. I had never made any effort to hide my disdain for her. She, on her part, never made any effort to hide her care and benevolence. That day too, she was elated upon seeing me. She paid for her vegetables, and we started walking together, arm in arm. Ten seconds into our conversation, she asked me why I was walking so slowly. I told her that that was my normal pace."

"When we reached her house – she had married a decent and well-off man by this time – she sat me down, brought a glass of water, and started asking questions. Did I feel any pain in my private parts; how frequent was it; when was the pain at its peak; did the soreness ever go; what kind of sexual relationship I had with my husband; did I ever enjoy sex; did he ever ask me before doing it… Once I was done answering her questions, she told me that he had been raping me all these years. The obvious question that came to my mind was – Isn't this how it is supposed to be? We are husband and wife, after all. And that was my introduction to marital rape."

"When did this happen?"

"A couple of years before we found you."

"Did you tell anyone?"

"Did I have anyone to tell? I don't have any surviving members of my family. Shyam is his father's son. I don't know how Shyam and Bina are in the bedroom, but I hope they are not like us. Though Bina and I have never had a proper conversation, I have never seen her walk the way I did all my life till Shyam's father was alive and virile. I could do nothing but receive all the information with a quiet comprehension of having lived as a helpless and unaware victim all my life."

"Did you confront Mukeshlal?"

"I did, but not aggressively. He'd just had a heart attack and had been hospitalised. I went to see him after my chance encounter with Meena. He was in a semi-conscious state with an oxygen mask on when I saw him. But I was feeling something inside me after a long, long time, and I had to say it to him."

"What did you say?"

"I told him that I wished him dead; that I'd kill him that very instant if I had the energy in me. I didn't have the energy in me because he had drained all of it. He had ruined me. He had attacked my very being and completely destroyed it. I had been reduced to an empty vessel, to something resembling a non-human; and he was the one responsible for it. I removed his oxygen mask and walked away."

"How did he survive?"

"He was lucky. His pulse had dropped drastically. He was in a very critical state when a nurse came to check on him. He was revived eventually."

"Do you regret that?"

"That he lived? No, not really. His heart attack and the short period of oxygen deficit had made him very weak and mentally very frail; he had lost bowel control and had become very incoherent towards the end, as you saw. The remaining few years of his life were excruciating for him. They had to be. He was no longer the authoritative and controlling head of the family that he earlier was. He had lost his power and prestige. I loved seeing him suffer. I wish he had suffered harder, and more. God called him too early."

It was a bright, sunny, winter morning, the air crisp but not sharp. I was lying on the grass in the front yard of the house, soaking up the early morning sun. It was 8 a.m. So, there was still some dew on the grass that hadn't completely evaporated. The slight dampness on my back and the soft caress of the wind on my face felt unusually calming. I could feel all my anxieties, troubles and worries evaporate with the dew, to be replaced with a strange lightness, and a stranger serenity. After a long time, I could hear my breathing and feel an emptiness in my chest. For a rare briefness, my mind let go of its burdens; I felt oddly weightless. I opened my eyes to the radiant, blue sky and its floating clouds. The sky was so impeccably clear that the clouds seemed canvassed on it. A couple of minutes later, inadvertently, I found myself feeling envious of the clouds. They were free, and miles away from this harrowing world; from *my* harrowing world. They were so white and unblemished. They seemed to be floating in the sky with contentment so surreal, it made me want to scream my throat sore at them. The only thread that pulled me back was the incomprehensibility of what to scream, how to scream and why.

"Tamanna!" There was no way I could be left alone to myself. I ran back inside, yelling in return, "What?"

"Where have you been?" asked Shyam.

"Outside, in the front yard."

"What were you doing there?"

"Lying."

"You were lying in the front yard at 8:30 in the morning?"

"Yes."

"Why?"

"Why not?"

"Because you're not living here for free!"

"Aren't Veda and Lakshman living here for free?"

"Are you comparing yourself to *them*?"

"Can't I? Legally, I too, am a daughter of this house."

"You are too smart for your own good. Yes, you may be a *daughter* of this house legally but don't fool yourself by what those papers say. You were a stranger when you came here, and you still are."

"You didn't know my name when I came here. But you do now. How am I a stranger now, in that case? Maybe *you* are too smart for your own good. At least, that is what you like to think so."

"Shut up!"

Shyam used to wear a lot of rings on his right hand, and that was the hand he slapped me with; with the back of it. "You are a nuisance to me, to this house and to this world. Since the day you entered my life, I have faced nothing but losses and failures. First, my father died. Then, I got demoted. The bills have increased because now I must provide for another person who doesn't even belong here. Veda and Lakshman have grown distant from their grandmother. *My* mother, who used to take care of no one but *us*, shifted all her attention to you.

My wife remains perpetually on the edge because of *you*. You brought nothing but unhappiness to this family! If I could, I'd throw you out this very instant. It's a shame that I can't. It's a shame that you are alive and still breathing under *my* roof."

With a cut face and sliced cheek, I somehow managed to drag myself to my room. I opened the drawer beside my bed and pulled out the Swiss knife that I used to keep there, hidden. I went to the other side of the bed, the one that faced the window, and sat down on the floor. Glancing at the open sky and the free clouds, wishing for it to be the last time, and remembering the peace I had felt that morning, I cut my wrist.

21

A NEW LIFE

I survived.

Death had rejected me – another place where I was not wanted.

My eyes opened to a sharp, white light shining on me. I jerked my head to the side to block the light, instead, my eyes fell on Shyam – leaning against the frame of the door, his arms crisscrossed, beating a pen on his arm in a constant rhythm and blankly glaring into the ceiling – standing with Bina – her feeble figure standing opposite to Shyam staring down at his shoes – at the entrance of the hospital ward.

My instant response to the sight of them was to immediately shut my eyes in a desperate attempt to believe that I was dead, and hallucinations can occur even after death. I strongly wanted to believe that I had killed myself, that I had finally succeeded at something, that I still had some control over my life, and that I had won for myself freedom from the people I had opened my eyes to that glum morning. But I hadn't; I had failed.

"Hey! Open your eyes!" Bina hissed at me. "What were you thinking before doing that? Now we have so many hospital bills to pay and the police to answer to as well. Why do you always have to make things difficult?"

"We'll have a talk once you're out of here. Make it soon," Shyam glared down at me.

I was discharged from the hospital the next day. All possible charges against me, for trying to take my life, and against Shyam, for child abuse, were dropped. Shyam was a corporate lawyer, and filthily rich. And if it's not evident, money can buy everything. His money kept me away from juvenile prison and bought him his innocence.

We did not have the talk that Shyam intended to do, chiefly because Dadi did not allow him to do it, and I was too adamant about not opening my mouth in front of him. He couldn't physically force me either. My face and wrist were already heavily bandaged. Another bruise by him and his money would have failed at keeping him safe.

1 November, Monday

11:30 p.m.

Dear Durga Di,

Where are you? I feel so alone here…all the time. Dadi tries to keep me company, but there's a limit to what she can do. That limit is decided by her son. Everything in this house is decided by him.

This family is not very different from ours. Even though they are much richer, their relations are pretty similar to what we grew up with. I don't want to talk about them, so I won't tell you exactly what the similarities are, but you must believe me when I say that I see our family in them. And it is not a pleasant sight, Durga Di…

There, I never felt alone, because I always had you by my side, I had my friends with me... But here, I have no one. I know what your reply would have been to this. You would have said, "You have YOU, Tamanna." But you know what? Sometimes, I feel as if I don't have me either. I feel like a stranger to myself. I feel like I have forgotten who I was before I came here. I feel like I'll never be able to remember who I was...

And it scares me, Durga Di... The thought of never meeting myself again, the thought of never knowing who or what I was, the thought of always remaining a stranger to myself... It is scary...

I don't want to stay like this, Durga Di. I don't want to stay scared. I feel trapped, caged in this fear. It is suffocating... so suffocating... it makes me want to scream, shout, cry, bang my head against the wall, punch the cupboard with my fist... But I'm scared... I'm scared that I won't hear anything... I'm scared that I won't feel anything... I'm scared that I won't feel pain – that I will bleed myself out till there is nothing left in me... Nothing.

3 November, Wednesday

11:45 p.m.

Dear Durga Di,

Every morning feels like a struggle. Opening my eyes to the blaring alarm clock feels the toughest. That first sigh after opening my eyes, which tells me that I'm not dead yet and that I'm unfortunate enough to have woken up to another miserable day in this miserable house, feels like a sharp knife has been inserted into my chest and is being twisted, round and round, again and again.

Today, when my alarm went off, I silenced it and made one strong attempt at hauling myself up from the bed.

I was half successful.

I lifted myself up and put my feet on the floor, and that's it… I couldn't move further. I felt stuck. Paralysed. As if my feet had been glued to the floor. As if all the muscles in my body had together refused to do their jobs. My hands were clutching the bedsheet and my eyes were staring straight ahead at the wall (I discovered a black dot on the wall today which I had never noticed before).

I did not know what to do. I kept staring at the wall. I could feel the pain in my hands from clutching the bedsheet; I knew that I was in my room; I knew that it was morning; I knew where the bathroom was, where the chairs were, where the cupboard was, where the bedside cabinet was, where the window was. I knew everything. I just didn't know what to DO.

I felt as though I was caught; caught somewhere in the middle, in that tiny space between knowing and not-knowing, between alive and not alive.

It was only when Dadi came to my room to call me for breakfast that I switched back to consciousness (I don't think I was unconscious though. I don't know what I was. I wish you were here to tell me.)

✳ ✳ ✳

Dear Durga Di,

I got slapped today. By Shyam. For accidentally spilling some tea on his new trousers. Well, you know, I'm used to slaps. I've been slapped so many times. But no one in our family wore so many rings on their fingers. Shyam wears four. He slapped me with the hand that had four rings. My face didn't stop bleeding for a good half an hour. Thank God, he didn't punch me though. That would have been so much worse.

✳ ✳ ✳

10 November, Wednesday

10:55 p.m.

Dear Durga Di,

Wishing you a very, very happy birthday!

I've been trying to keep myself happy since morning by thinking about all your birthdays that we spent together. Remember, I once stole a cupcake for you? Everybody had forgotten that it was your birthday; even Ma. So, she didn't give you any money. You were so sad that day. But I didn't have money either. So, we celebrated your birthday under the mango tree by pretending to blow out a candle and cut the cake with an imaginary knife, and then actually feeding it to each other.

But my favourite has to be your eleventh birthday. Do you know why? Because Papa didn't come home the whole day! We didn't have to see his face for a full 24 hours! Wow! That was probably one of the best days of my life too. We spent the morning and afternoon together, walking around, talking; Dadu gave you two big chocolates; Ma had made kheer for you; Rahul Bhaiya and Naveen had also behaved themselves. You were so happy that day... WE were so happy...

There's more that I want to write, but I feel so tired today. I tried keeping myself happy the entire day today. But I couldn't. Each memory, each thought ended with a heaviness in my chest. This heaviness is not a new feeling. You know that. But this one was still different; because I couldn't remove it.

Today, in the afternoon, when everybody was resting, I came to my room and locked the door. I remember that you told me once – "Tamanna, our hearts are like clouds. They need to empty themselves to make space for more."

I thought that maybe I needed to cry and that crying would make the heaviness go away. But... Durga Di, I couldn't cry. Not even a drop. The heaviness just kept increasing, until the time I could feel it in my throat. Still, the tears didn't come out.

The heaviness felt unbearable. After a point, I couldn't even breathe. I didn't know what was happening to me. I couldn't think. All I felt was a violent need to cry!

So, I put my hands around my neck, and strangled myself, piercing my nails into the sides of my neck.

It was painful. But also comforting.

I finally cried.

✳ ✳ ✳

13 November, Saturday

11:45 p.m.

Dear Durga Di,

Today was a really strange day.

Usually, when I wake up in the morning, I feel drained, like an orange with its juice sucked out. But today, I couldn't understand. So, I just got up from bed and began my day as I normally did.

Again, on most days, I feel tired, or frustrated, or angry, or hopeless, or smash-his-head-on-the-wall violent, or pull-out-her-hair irritated; some other days, I feel so alone, I hold both my hands together to feel as if there's someone holding me. But today, I went about my day feeling nothing. Imagine a human-like machine working and walking around in the house. That.

You know what? I've been thinking about what to write next for the past 10 minutes, but there are no words in my head. I think I'll just sleep.

Good night, Durga Di.

*** * ***

17 November, Tuesday

11:55 p.m.

Dear Durga Di,

Do you think there is a purpose behind everyone's existence in this world? Do you think it's their purpose that makes their existence worthwhile? That it's this purpose that adds value to their life? That their existence is dependent on other people? That their worth is decided by how valuable they are to other people?

But what if someone does not have a purpose? Does it make their life, their existence worthless? If they are of no use, no value to other people, does it mean they are useless? Value-less? What happens to such people, Durga Di? Do they live on, like garbage waiting to be disposed of? Or do they die, because whether living or dead doesn't matter?

Why do people need a purpose for their existence? Why can they not exist without a value attached to them? Why do we need to lead our lives in an attempt to constantly prove our worth to others? A worth that cares more about itself in relation to other people; a worth that is constantly trying to prove its worth – a worth that feels like a burden if it fails to prove itself.

I don't know why I'm alive, Durga Di. Probably that's why I'm babbling about existence; probably because I can't see any reason for it. I keep asking myself – "Why am I here? What am I doing here? Does anyone even need me here?"

But I never find answers. Somehow, I always get lost in the questions. It's like a maze, a dark, tunnel-like maze. I don't know how I get inside. Does someone push me inside it? Or do I just walk into it myself? I don't think it matters as much as why I'm unable to get out.

It's endless, Durga Di. I keep walking and walking and walking, but I never reach the end. And you know, it gets so scary sometimes, it is so dark. Always. Utter darkness. Like a thick, black blanket. No light.

✳ ✳ ✳

20 November, Friday

11:30 p.m.

Dear Durga Di,

Love is a really frustrating emotion. No, I don't have a boyfriend. Not even a crush. I'm talking about normal love – the love that we have for each other, the love that holds a friendship together, the love that makes a grandmother confide in her granddaughter, the love that glistens in the eyes of a mother upon holding her baby for the first time...

I'm not rambling this time. I was thinking about my friends - Eva, Eric, Nazia, Taheera, and Vihaan. I love them, Durga Di. I love them so much. I try not to think about them because each time I do, I start crying. Sometimes, I start crying in from of THEM! I hate it! I don't like being weak in front of them! I don't want them to know how weak I feel sometimes! But I can't help it! I want to see my friends! I want to meet them! I want to talk to them! I want to play with them! I want to cry with them! I want to walk around with them! I want to study with them! I want them back, Durga Di... I just want them back...

✳ ✳ ✳

21 November, Saturday

11:10 p.m.

Dear Durga Di,

I could not finish my last entry. I fell asleep, crying, on my diary. I'll tell you why I think love is a frustrating emotion.

When I arrived here, within a couple of days, I understood that there was no one even close to tolerable here. Except for one. Dadi.

Dadi takes care of me. She looks after me. She is there for me when no one else is. She gives me love when everybody is busy hating me. She showed me what a grandparent's love is. She showed me how it feels to be loved by a grandparent.

I love Dadi. She is one of the purest people I have met, Durga Di. She reminds me of Dadu. Every time I sit with her, talk to her, sleep on her lap, cry in her arms, I am reminded of Dadu. It was very painful in the beginning; Dadu's memory is something I had intended to erase. But each time Dadi smiled at me, I was reminded of the pain of being separated from Dadu, the pain of his memory, the pain of his death. I decided to distance myself from Dadi, to protect myself from the pain. But I couldn't. There was no way I could keep her away from me for too long.

She has a way of loving people, you know. She loves them not for who or what they are, but because she knows that every human being is deserving of love. Her love is not conditional; one does not have to be a certain way to earn her love. Her love is abundant, available for all...they just need to accept it.

Initially, I was trying to not accept it, to not fall for the trap that I had started thinking love was. But I failed. I had to, right? It is not possible for anyone to resist the strength of her love for long. Then how could I?

It is frustrating, Durga Di. The more you love someone, the more pain that love is likely to cause you. Dadi has been keeping unwell for the last few days. I have been taking care of her, but nobody here cares! Shyam keeps forgetting to call the doctor, and his wife is lost in her own world. Her own grandchildren are least bothered. There is nothing I can do…

I can't lose her too, Durga Di… I can't…

✳ ✳ ✳

I lost her. Dadi. She died today at 11.

✳ ✳ ✳

1 December, Tuesday

11:40 p.m.

Dear Durga Di

A week has gone by since I lost Dadi. A week of once again feeling the way I felt on that evening when I got separated from my friends on entering the city.

I have barely stepped out of my room this whole week. Whenever I do, I feel my mouth drying up, my stomach turning, my heart beating almost out of my chest, my jaw quivering… I was so confused the first time it happened. But I realised the next day that it always starts with the first step I take out of my room. And it made sense then.

Durga Di, do you think I'll be able to get over her? Over her death? Over her absence?

*** * ***

6 December, Monday

10:30 p.m.

Dear Durga Di,

I cannot understand this family. It has been barely two weeks since Dadi's death and everything's normal here! Everyone is behaving as if nothing happened, as if no one died, as if one member of the family is not less, as if no one's mother or grandmother passed away. EVERYTHING IS NORMAL!

It is so strange. Dadi used to work so much around the house – she would pack Veda and Lakshman's lunch boxes, set out their uniforms in the morning, get them dressed for school, make Shyam's lunch, make breakfast in the morning, organise the kitchen, look after the servants if any of them ever got sick, take care of the house's medicine stock. She would even prepare dinner if Bina was out for a day out or at a party with her friends. Dadi was almost always, in some way or the other, needed to run the household. And now that she is no more, one would expect the whole house to crumble down. But no! Everything is functioning perfectly well! Breakfast, lunch, dinner; the servants; the kitchen; everything is fine.

It didn't take any of them long to return to their normal lives.

Dead or alive, she didn't matter to them. She dedicated her entire life to them, Durga Di. This family was her whole world. But did she receive anything in return? No. Nothing. Not even grief.

✳ ✳ ✳

9 December, Thursday

11:55 p.m.

I open my eyes in the morning
To the dazzling sun waiting on me,
Or to the light raindrops knocking on my window,
Or to the coy wind teasing the leaves.

I look out the (my?) window
And I'm greeted by the lushness of the trees,
The youthfulness of the flowers,
The music of children's laughter,
The chatter of the birds;
The shopkeeper across the road and his radio,
The graffiti on the walls screaming 'Freedom!'

I turn towards the (my?) mirror
And I look at myself.
I look at my eyes,
Eyes which have seen smiles;
I look at my ears,
Ears which have heard so many stories;
I look at my hair,

Hair which has been pulled in playful banter;
I put my hand on my chest
To feel the beat within
Of the heart that has felt happiness
That has felt love and has loved.
I touch my lips,
Lips that have felt Ma's forehead,
Lips that have kissed flowers and the dusty pages of books.
I look at my hands –
Hands that have helped and healed
Hands that have written, drawn and painted
Hands that have created.

I look at myself
I look at me.
I look at the world outside
I look at the morning,
And I feel happy,
I try to feel happy,
I want to feel happy,
Badly, desperately,
I want to feel happy.
I want to know it.
Happiness? Happiness.

26 December, Monday

11:55 p.m.

Dear Durga Di,

I got married yesterday. Surprised, right? Me too. I am married to a man I barely know. He is not even a man; he is just twenty-two. But he is still so older than me. I don't really care, you know. No one asked me before meeting with this family; no one asked me before finalising the marriage; no one asked me before taking me to the court; no one asked me before handing me the documents. And frankly, I didn't care. I kept doing whatever was asked of me, without thinking. I went to the court, accepted the documents when they were handed to me, took the pen when it was offered, and signed the papers. Without thinking. Almost unconsciously. I can't even recall the colour of the folder the documents were in. All I remember thinking is – 'Why is he not saying anything?'

By 'he,' I mean my husband (I can't believe I have a husband now). He seemed as uncaring and unbothered as I was. I asked him yesterday, at night. Turns out, he hates his family, and he plans on moving away from them after earning his Master's degree and getting a stable job. I asked him, "What about me? Where will I live?" His reply was, "You'll come with me. You can finish your education if you want. We can even get a divorce if either of us feels like the marriage is not working out."

The conversation we had next... you'd want to know. So here it goes:

"There's something you should know about."

"Yes?"

I showed him my wrist. "I attempted suicide when I was a little above sixteen. It was right after another one of his accusations at me for ruining his life."

He held my wrist, very lightly, as if he was holding a delicate flower, and took a closer look at it. He went into a trance for half a minute, before I clicked my fingers in front of him. Very carefully, he put my wrist down, as though it were too fragile to even be held for long, and sat down in front of me.

"What was it that he said, that finally pushed you to that line?"

"It was nothing new. His old, redundant claims. But I reached my saturation. There was only a limit till which I could endure people saying how worthless I was. My limit broke that day." Silence. He sat there, his hands clasped together, staring at the floor, deep in some contemplation.

"I'll understand if you want to leave me after knowing about this. Just don't tell THEM. I'll leave first thing in the morning. No one will ever come to know anything."

He glanced up, and gazing straight into my eyes, said with a strange conviction, "I'm never leaving you. I don't care if we never establish a conjugal relationship. But I'd still like to be a part of your life, in whatever capacity you allow me. That's my promise to you."

Durga Di, I want to believe him. His voice was so steady when he said this; his eyes carried an uncanny certainty; he sounded so strong in that moment, and his promise, full of faith. I really want to believe him. But can I? Should I? What if he leaves too? What if he too hurts me? I'm tired of getting hurt, Durga Di… I'm just tired…

22

MY LIFE

My life had stopped making sense to me. No amount of thinking and reasoning could possibly explain why I was alive. Wrenched out of my village and estranged from my friends, there was nothing that remained of my past except my name. *Tamanna.* Desire, hope, wish. It's a beautiful word, and I have always loved my name. It reminded me to not let go of the light inside of me even when I was gripped by the darkest, thickest pall; it reminded me that the night is always followed by the dawn; and that no matter how strong a thunderstorm I'm hit by, the clouds will clear and the sun will shine again. But, after the 1991 riots and my induction into the new family, for the longest time, I felt disconnected from my name, as though it were somebody else's; as though I was somebody else.

My foster parents married me off when I turned eighteen. It wasn't elaborate or celebratory in any way; it was a court marriage. Neither did they care where they were marrying me off, nor did I care about who I was marrying. I had met my husband only once before the day of the wedding and never exchanged a word with him. The singular time we met, was with our parents over dinner. Both of us knew the exact purpose behind that dinner, but neither of us could care less about it. I had grown indifferent to everything around me: people, events, situations… No matter how grave a situation, it was received by me with a numbness that could be felt almost physically.

But I am a different person now. I am a wife and a mother of two brilliant children. All these years, I have been a good wife and a good mother. I love my family and I love the life that I have created for myself. Settling down after years of instability and feelings of whirring out of control, the sense of security felt strange; almost alien. But my husband made me comfortable in it. He constructed an ecosystem in which there was understanding, compassion and empathy; which exuded warmth, comfort and love; and he placed me in the centre of this ecosystem. He provided the contentment that I had lost when I lost my friends.

When I became a mother, I discovered another self of me, a self that was nurturing, strong for someone else and resilient – a self that learnt to acknowledge the meaning of unconditional love. The first time, when I received the news of my pregnancy, I was scared. I never had ideal parent figures around me when I was young – my father was an abusive alcoholic, and my mother a sacrificial lamb. I did not know what an ideal parent was like. But I soon realised that this was not a restriction, but an opportunity – an opportunity to become something that did not carry the burden of the past. Motherhood gave me a chance to navigate my way through the unknown, unexplored territory of parenthood. It gave me a chance to be someone untethered by the norms of "idealness."

But I could never be a friend again; I never found my friends. Did they live? Or are they dead? If they died, how did they die? Was it a painful death, or was it the kind that slowly, painlessly lures you in and traps you when you least expect it? If they are alive, what kind of lives are they living? Are they truly living, or is it another feeble opposition to death? Are they happy in their lives, or are they craving death? Do they still think of death as their ultimate refuge? Or has the thrill of life replaced the longing for death?

I spent my life fulfilling every role that I encountered and undertook. But somewhere along this path, I forgot to fulfil the role I owed to myself; I forgot to reclaim myself. The disjunct I had felt with my name during my teen years and at the time of my wedding, has now taken an inconspicuous, but permanent seat in my life. *Tamanna.* Desire, hope, wish. Desire for? Hope for? Wish for? I do not have answers for these. Is it a desire to find me and my friends? A hope that I'll be able to relive the moments I spent with them? A wish for building a life less troubled and more complete?

Tamanna.

9 798890 669148